MYSTERIE

#2 The **Nighttime Cabin Thief**

A Mystery about Light

by Lynda Beauregard

illustrated by Der-shing Helmer

GRAPHIC UNIVERSE™ • MINNEAPOLIS • NEW YORK

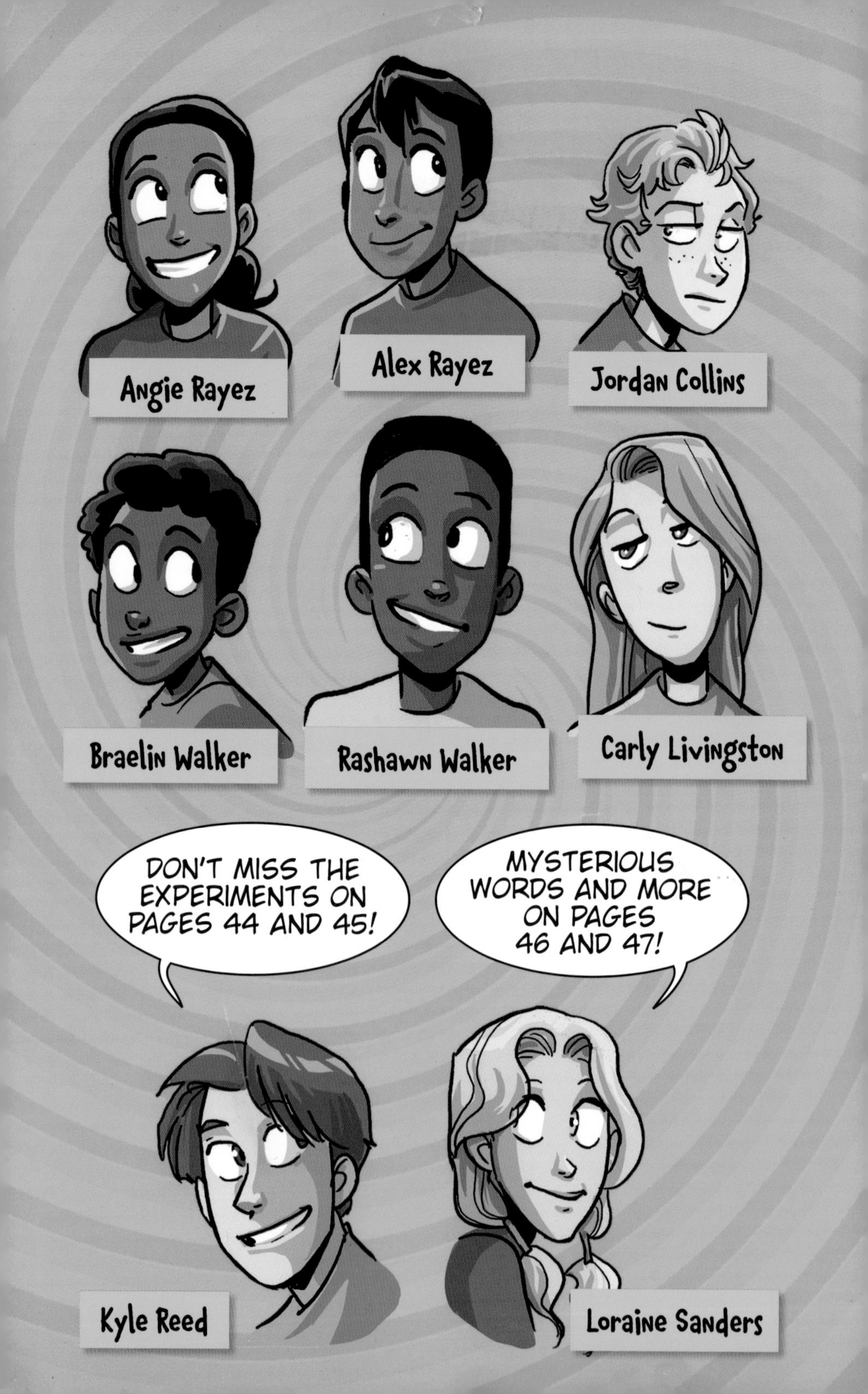
Angie Rayez
Alex Rayez
Jordan Collins
Braelin Walker
Rashawn Walker
Carly Livingston
DON'T MISS THE EXPERIMENTS ON PAGES 44 AND 45!
MYSTERIOUS WORDS AND MORE ON PAGES 46 AND 47!
Kyle Reed
Loraine Sanders

Light is a form of energy.

Light travels in waves and moves in straight lines. When light hits an object, the density (compactness) and color of the object determine whether the light bends, bounces off the object, is absorbed by the object, or passes right through it. When light passes through a lens, it can make objects look bigger or smaller than they really are.

Light bounces (reflects) off shiny surfaces such as mirrors. When you look in a mirror, you are seeing the light wave being reflected back exactly as it hit the mirror. Dull, dark objects absorb light rather than reflecting it back. Some substances, including water, bend light waves as the light passes through them.

Story by Lynda Beauregard
Illustrations by Der-shing Helmer
Coloring by Jenn Manley Lee
Lettering by Marshall Dillon

Graphic Universe™
A division of Lerner Publishing Group, Inc.
241 First Avenue North
Minneapolis, MN 55401 U.S.A.

Website address: www.lernerbooks.com

Main body text set in CCWildwords.
Typeface provided by Comicraft/Active Images.

Library of Congress Cataloging-in-Publication Data

Beauregard, Lynda.
    The nighttime cabin thief : a mystery about light / by Lynda Beauregard ;
    illustrated by Der-shing Helmer.
        p. cm. — (Summer camp science mysteries)
        Summary: When several campers at Camp Dakota report missing items and
    begin pointing fingers at a fellow camper, a group of children search for the culprit.
    Includes glossary and experiments.
        ISBN: 978-0-7613-5692-9 (lib. bdg. : alk. paper)
        ISBN: 978-0-7613-8747-3 (eBook)
        1. Graphic novels. [1. Graphic novels. 2. Camps—Fiction. 3. Light—Fiction.]
    I. Helmer, Der-shing, ill. II. Title.
    PZ7.7.B42Ni 2012
    741.5'973—dc23   2011016593

Manufactured in the United States of America
2 –PP – 4/1/13

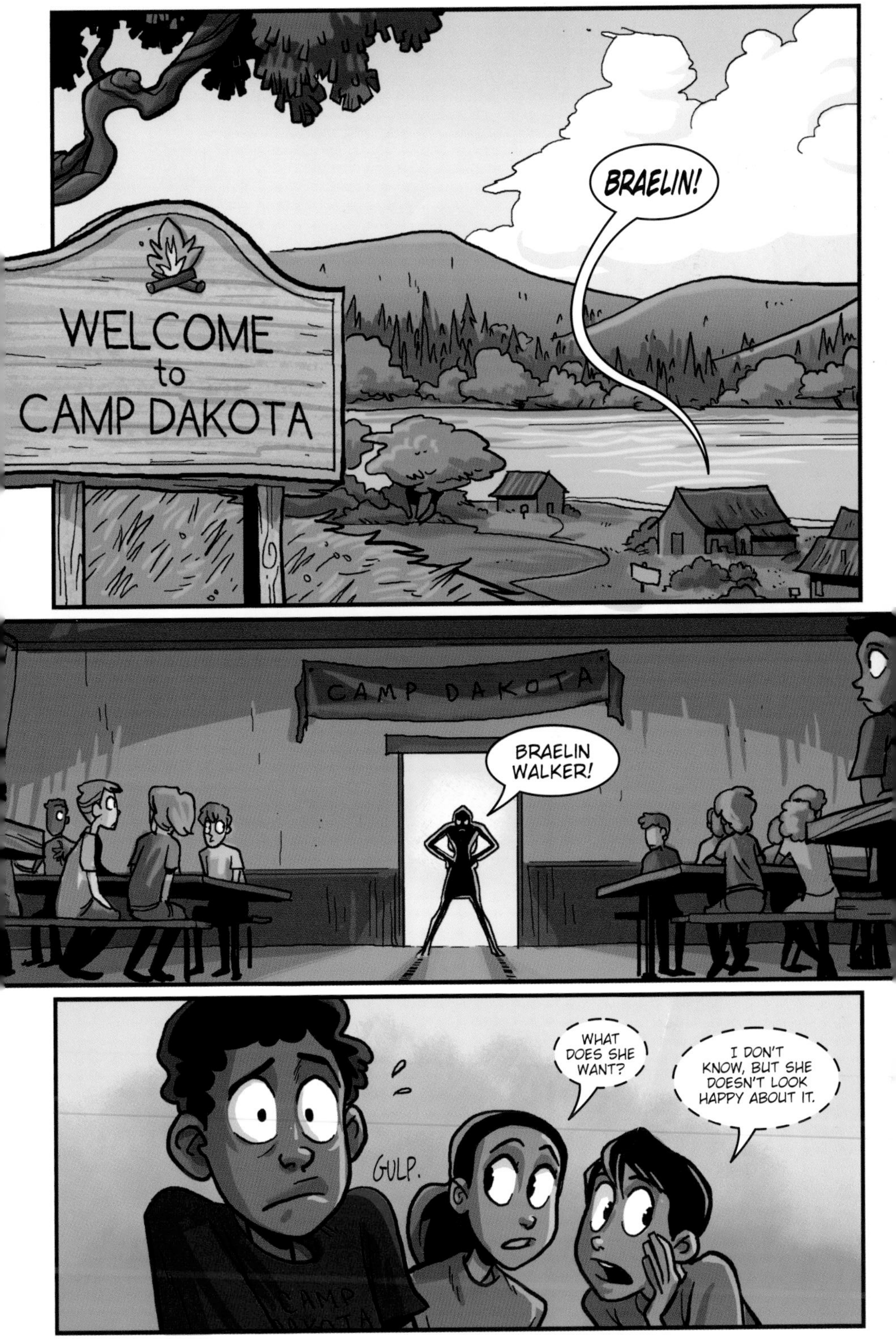
WELCOME
to
CAMP DAKOTA
BRAELIN!
CAMP DAKOTA
BRAELIN WALKER!
WHAT DOES SHE WANT?
GULP.
I DON'T KNOW, BUT SHE DOESN'T LOOK HAPPY ABOUT IT.

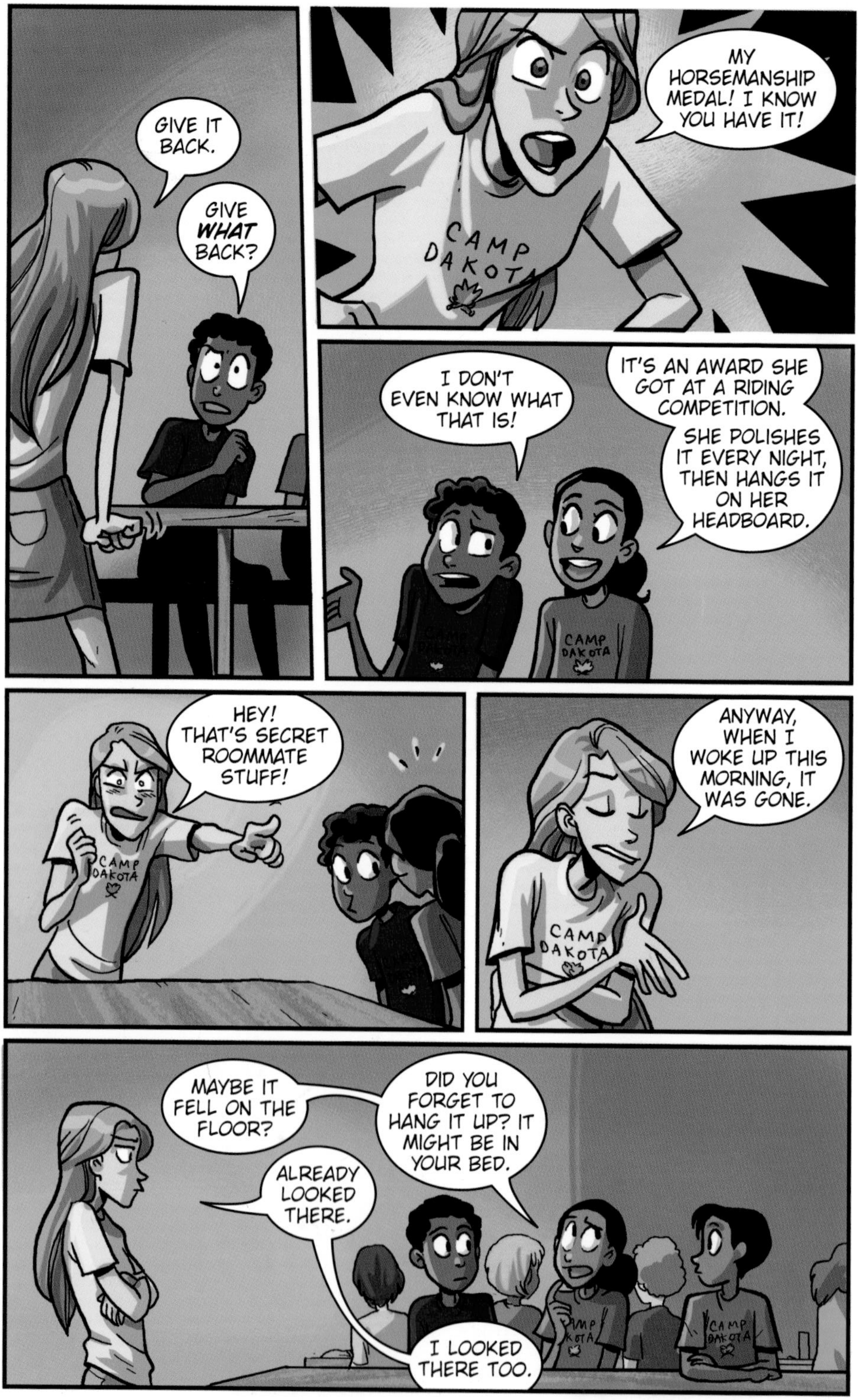
GIVE IT BACK.
GIVE *WHAT* BACK?
MY HORSEMANSHIP MEDAL! I KNOW YOU HAVE IT!
CAMP DAKOTA
I DON'T EVEN KNOW WHAT THAT IS!
IT'S AN AWARD SHE GOT AT A RIDING COMPETITION.
SHE POLISHES IT EVERY NIGHT, THEN HANGS IT ON HER HEADBOARD.
CAMP DAKOTA
HEY! THAT'S SECRET ROOMMATE STUFF!
CAMP DAKOTA
ANYWAY, WHEN I WOKE UP THIS MORNING, IT WAS GONE.
CAMP DAKOTA
MAYBE IT FELL ON THE FLOOR?
DID YOU FORGET TO HANG IT UP? IT MIGHT BE IN YOUR BED.
ALREADY LOOKED THERE.
I LOOKED THERE TOO.
CAMP DAKOTA

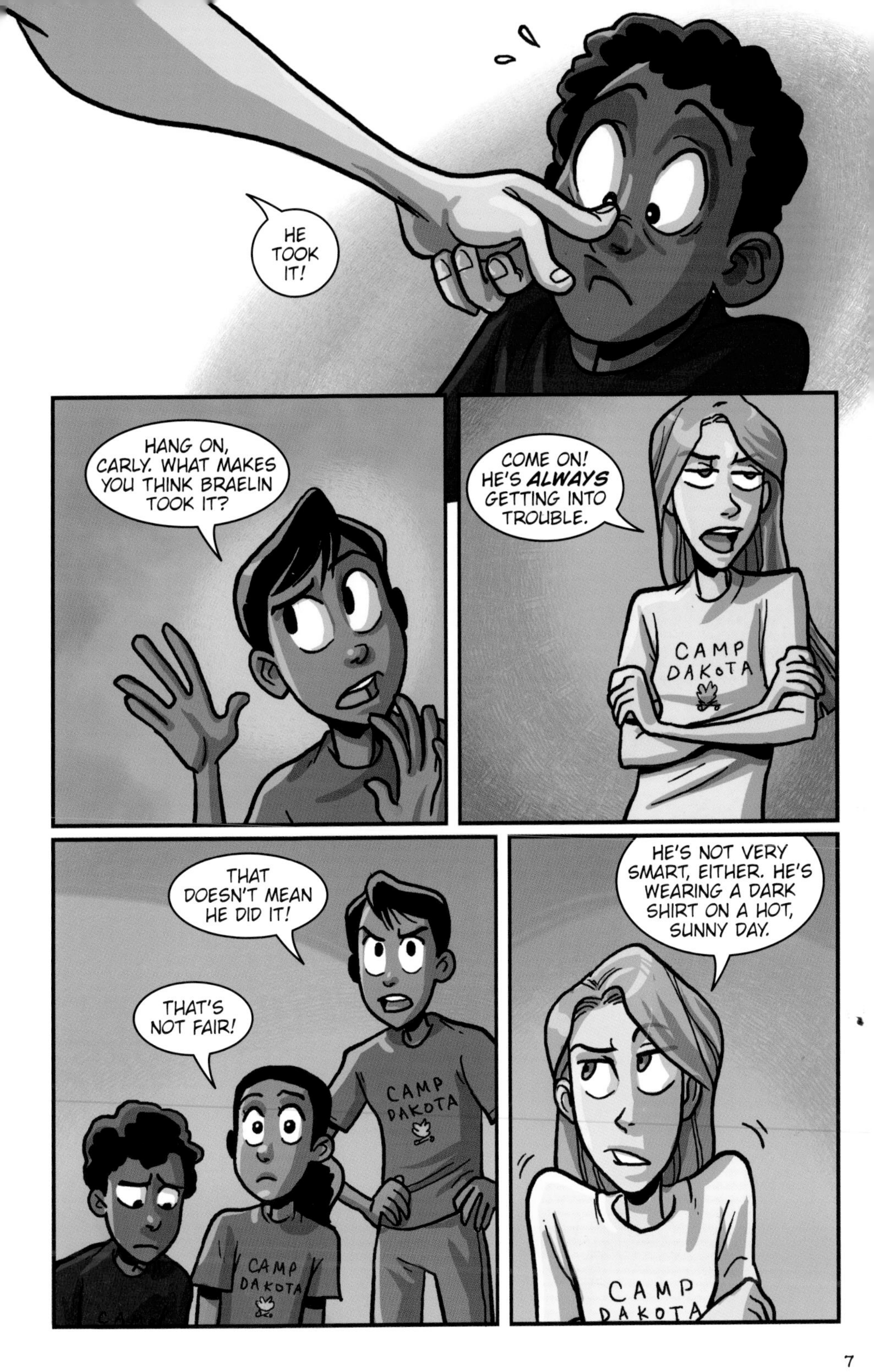
HE TOOK IT!
HANG ON, CARLY. WHAT MAKES YOU THINK BRAELIN TOOK IT?
COME ON! HE'S **ALWAYS** GETTING INTO TROUBLE.
CAMP DAKOTA
THAT DOESN'T MEAN HE DID IT!
THAT'S NOT FAIR!
CAMP DAKOTA
CAMP DAKOTA
HE'S NOT VERY SMART, EITHER. HE'S WEARING A DARK SHIRT ON A HOT, SUNNY DAY.
CAMP DAKOTA

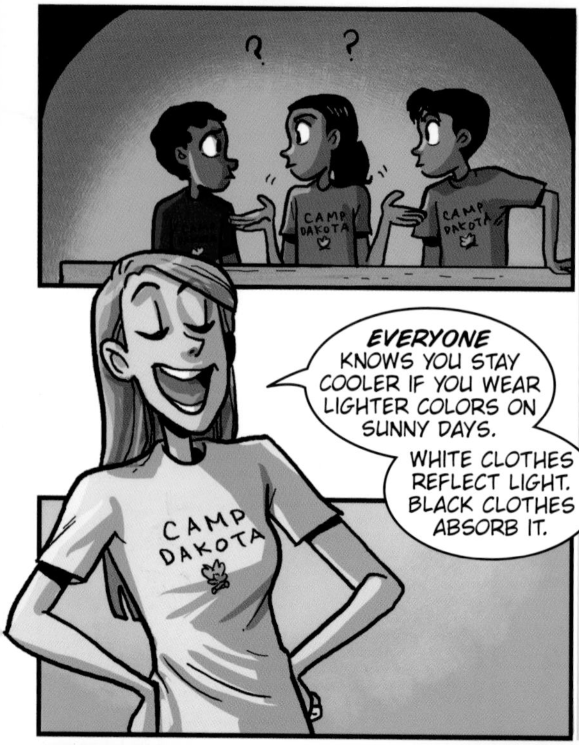
? ?
EVERYONE KNOWS YOU STAY COOLER IF YOU WEAR LIGHTER COLORS ON SUNNY DAYS.
WHITE CLOTHES REFLECT LIGHT. BLACK CLOTHES ABSORB IT.
CAMP DAKOTA

Light turns into heat when it strikes objects. Because white objects reflect light, very little light becomes heat after hitting the objects. Black objects absorb light instead of reflecting it, so they also absorb more heat.

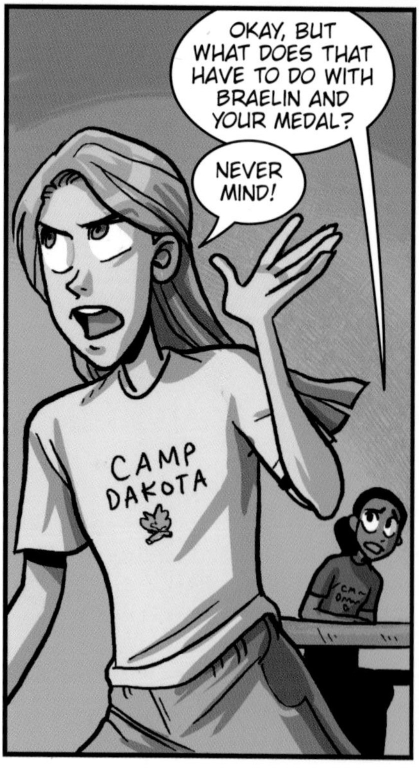
OKAY, BUT WHAT DOES THAT HAVE TO DO WITH BRAELIN AND YOUR MEDAL?
NEVER MIND!
CAMP DAKOTA

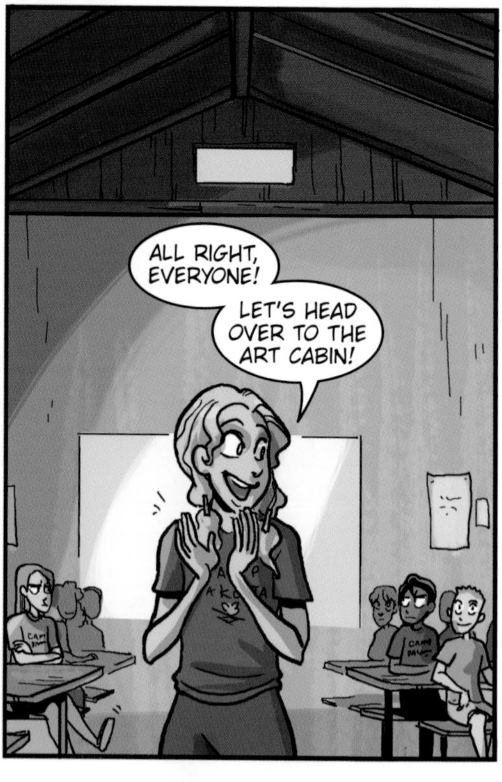
ALL RIGHT, EVERYONE!
LET'S HEAD OVER TO THE ART CABIN!

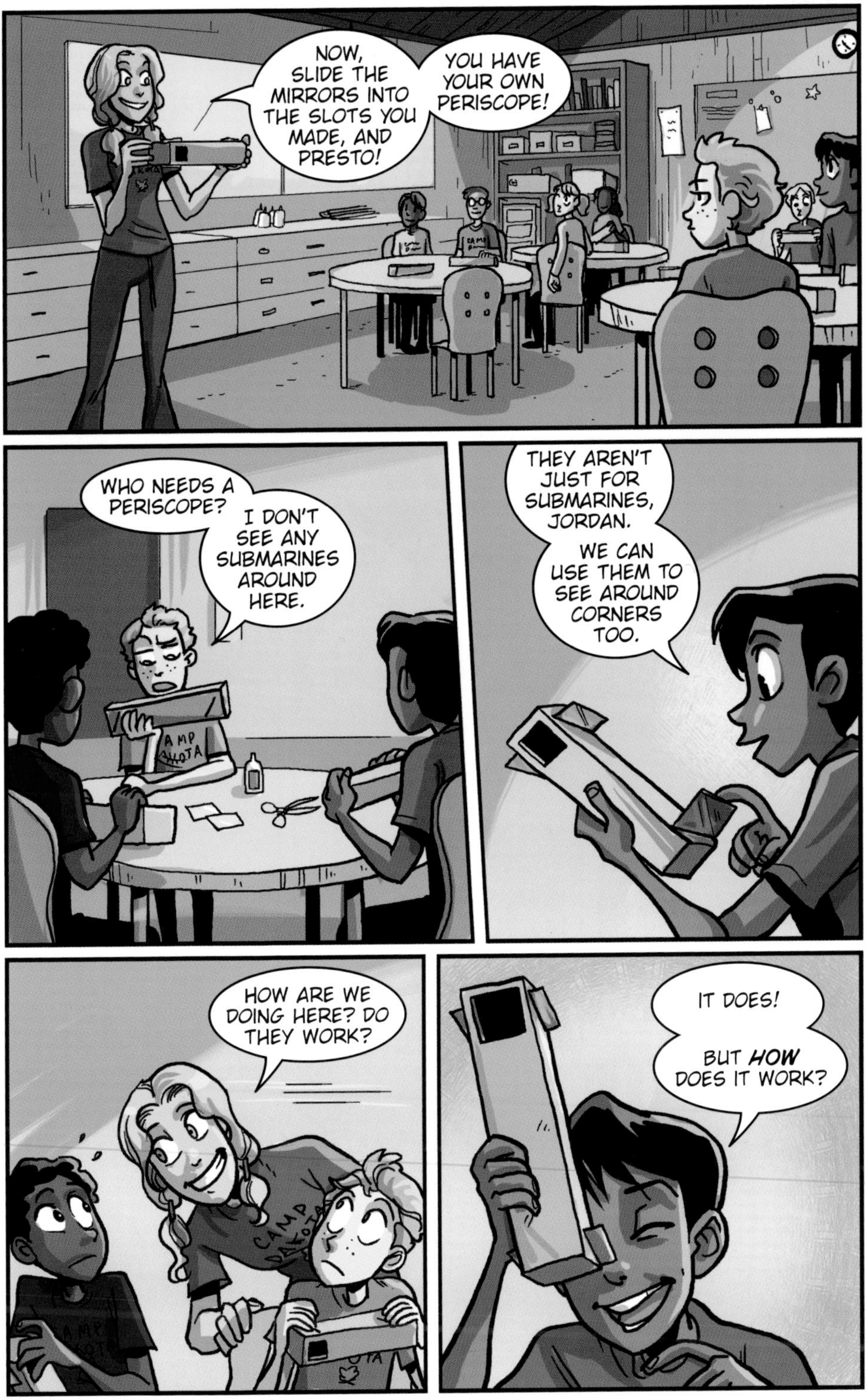
NOW, SLIDE THE MIRRORS INTO THE SLOTS YOU MADE, AND PRESTO!
YOU HAVE YOUR OWN PERISCOPE!
WHO NEEDS A PERISCOPE?
I DON'T SEE ANY SUBMARINES AROUND HERE.
THEY AREN'T JUST FOR SUBMARINES, JORDAN.
WE CAN USE THEM TO SEE AROUND CORNERS TOO.
HOW ARE WE DOING HERE? DO THEY WORK?
IT DOES!
BUT ***HOW*** DOES IT WORK?

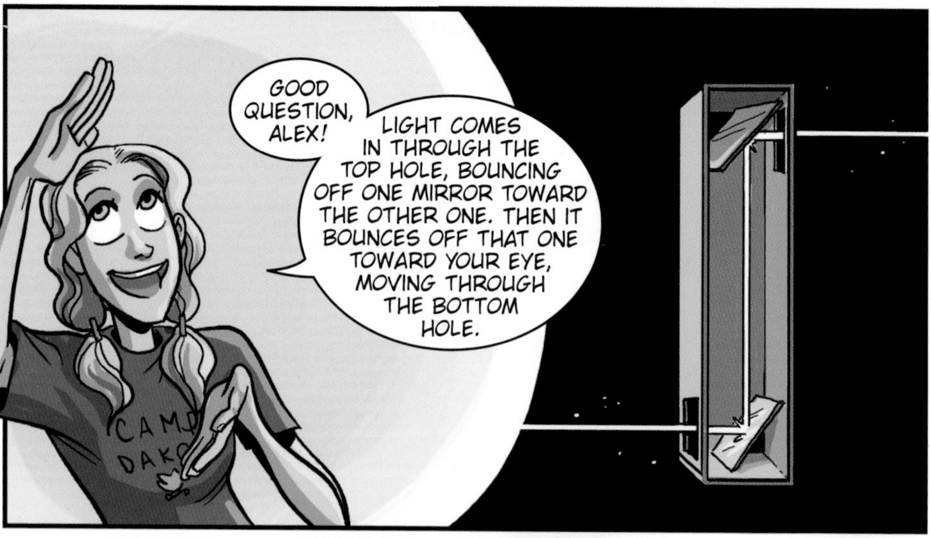
GOOD QUESTION, ALEX!
LIGHT COMES IN THROUGH THE TOP HOLE, BOUNCING OFF ONE MIRROR TOWARD THE OTHER ONE. THEN IT BOUNCES OFF THAT ONE TOWARD YOUR EYE, MOVING THROUGH THE BOTTOM HOLE.
CAMP DAKO

When light hits a shiny surface, like a mirror, the light reflects off the surface in the same pattern as when it made contact. Dull surfaces will scatter light in all directions when it bounces off them.

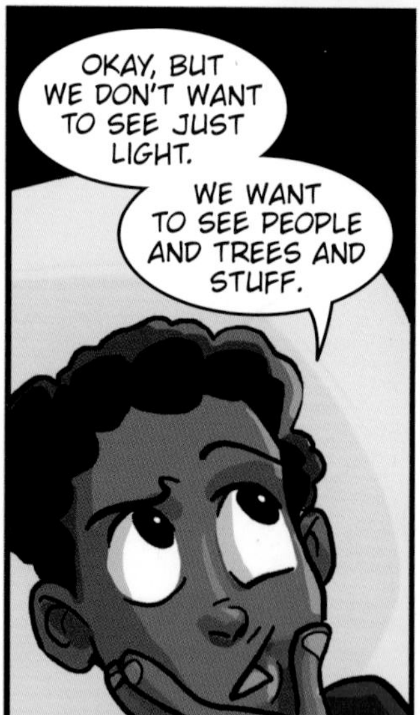
OKAY, BUT WE DON'T WANT TO SEE JUST LIGHT.
WE WANT TO SEE PEOPLE AND TREES AND STUFF.

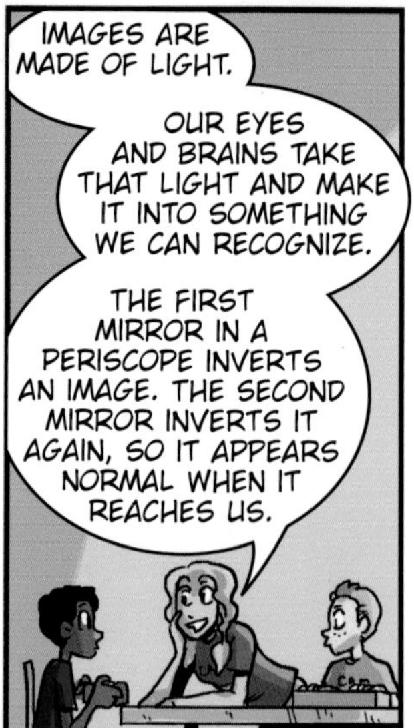
IMAGES ARE MADE OF LIGHT.
OUR EYES AND BRAINS TAKE THAT LIGHT AND MAKE IT INTO SOMETHING WE CAN RECOGNIZE.
THE FIRST MIRROR IN A PERISCOPE INVERTS AN IMAGE. THE SECOND MIRROR INVERTS IT AGAIN, SO IT APPEARS NORMAL WHEN IT REACHES US.

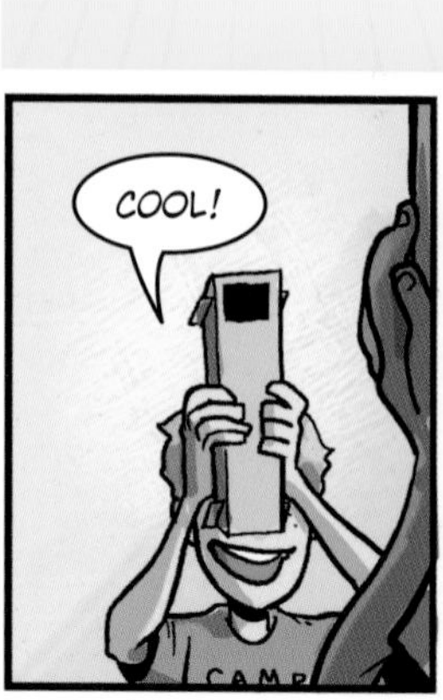
COOL!

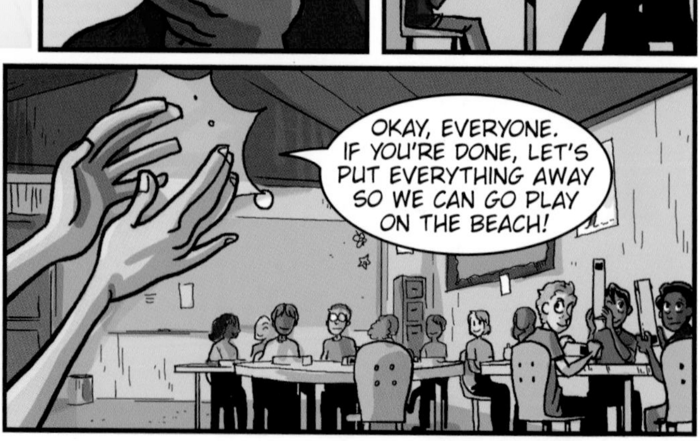
OKAY, EVERYONE. IF YOU'RE DONE, LET'S PUT EVERYTHING AWAY SO WE CAN GO PLAY ON THE BEACH!

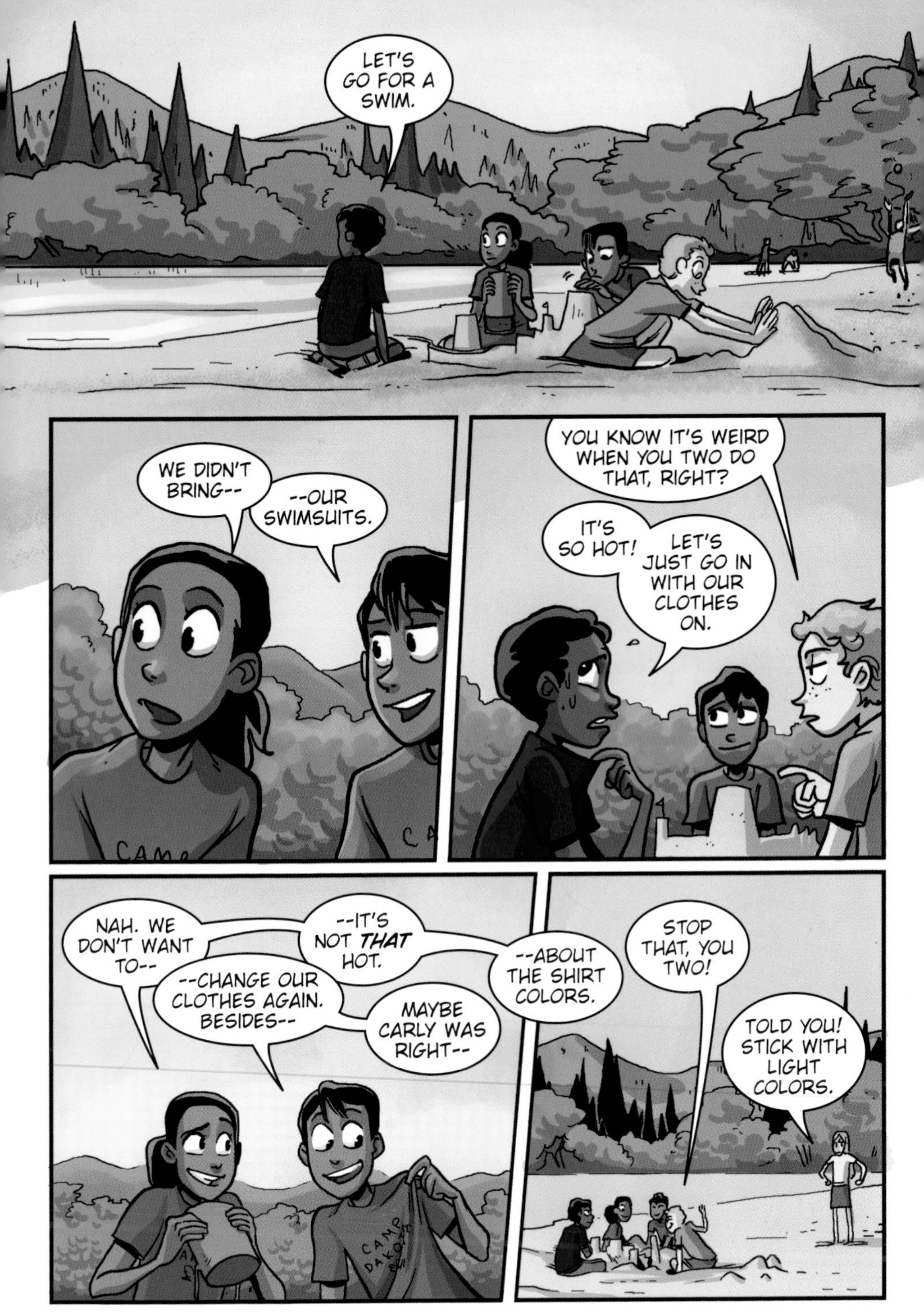
LET'S GO FOR A SWIM.
WE DIDN'T BRING--
--OUR SWIMSUITS.
YOU KNOW IT'S WEIRD WHEN YOU TWO DO THAT, RIGHT?
IT'S SO HOT!
LET'S JUST GO IN WITH OUR CLOTHES ON.
NAH. WE DON'T WANT TO--
--CHANGE OUR CLOTHES AGAIN. BESIDES--
--IT'S NOT *THAT* HOT.
MAYBE CARLY WAS RIGHT--
--ABOUT THE SHIRT COLORS.
STOP THAT, YOU TWO!
TOLD YOU! STICK WITH LIGHT COLORS.

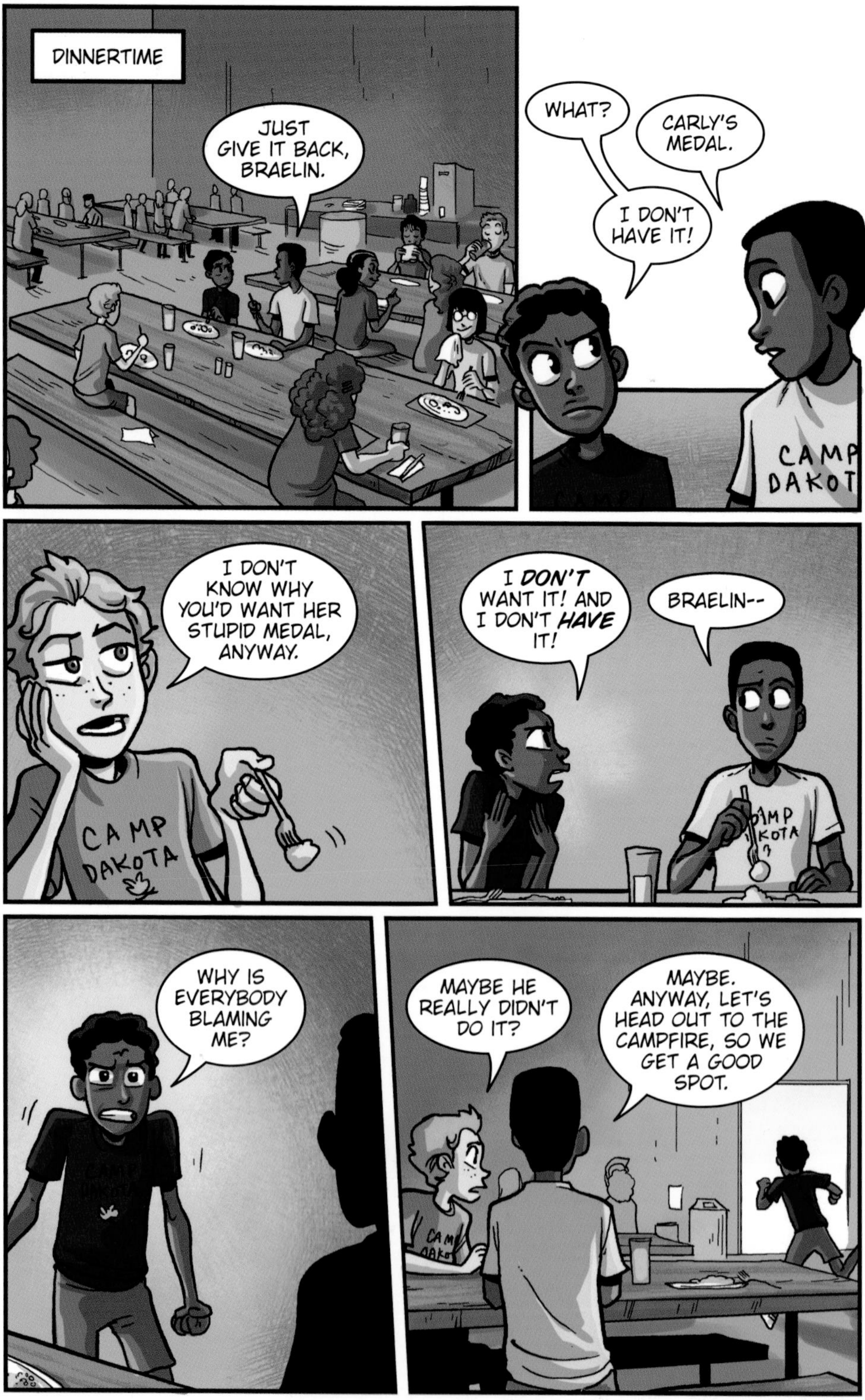
DINNERTIME
JUST GIVE IT BACK, BRAELIN.
WHAT?
CARLY'S MEDAL.
I DON'T HAVE IT!
I DON'T KNOW WHY YOU'D WANT HER STUPID MEDAL, ANYWAY.
I DON'T WANT IT! AND I DON'T HAVE IT!
BRAELIN--
WHY IS EVERYBODY BLAMING ME?
MAYBE HE REALLY DIDN'T DO IT?
MAYBE. ANYWAY, LET'S HEAD OUT TO THE CAMPFIRE, SO WE GET A GOOD SPOT.

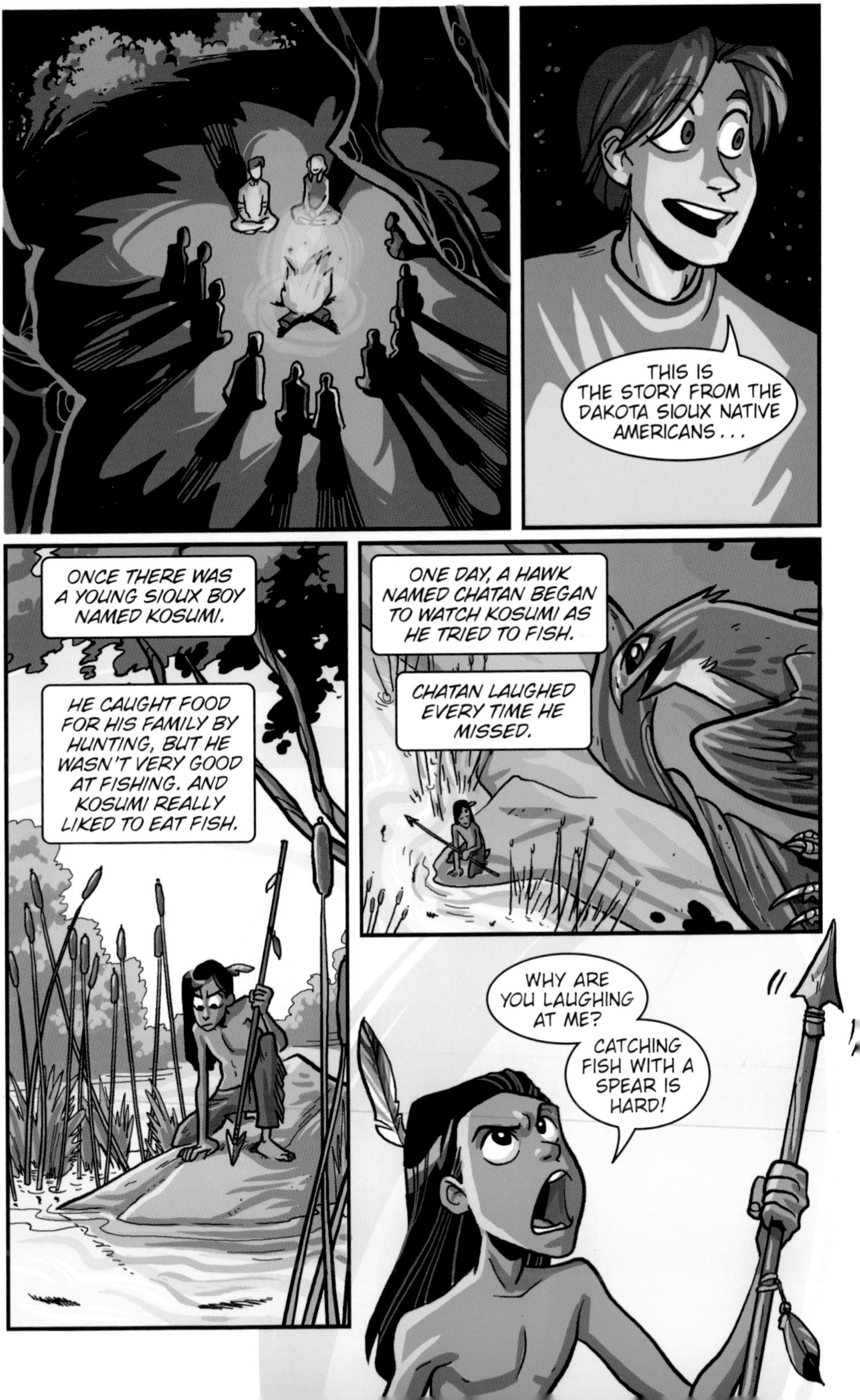
THIS IS THE STORY FROM THE DAKOTA SIOUX NATIVE AMERICANS . . .
ONCE THERE WAS A YOUNG SIOUX BOY NAMED KOSUMI.
HE CAUGHT FOOD FOR HIS FAMILY BY HUNTING, BUT HE WASN'T VERY GOOD AT FISHING. AND KOSUMI REALLY LIKED TO EAT FISH.
ONE DAY, A HAWK NAMED CHATAN BEGAN TO WATCH KOSUMI AS HE TRIED TO FISH.
CHATAN LAUGHED EVERY TIME HE MISSED.
WHY ARE YOU LAUGHING AT ME?
CATCHING FISH WITH A SPEAR IS HARD!

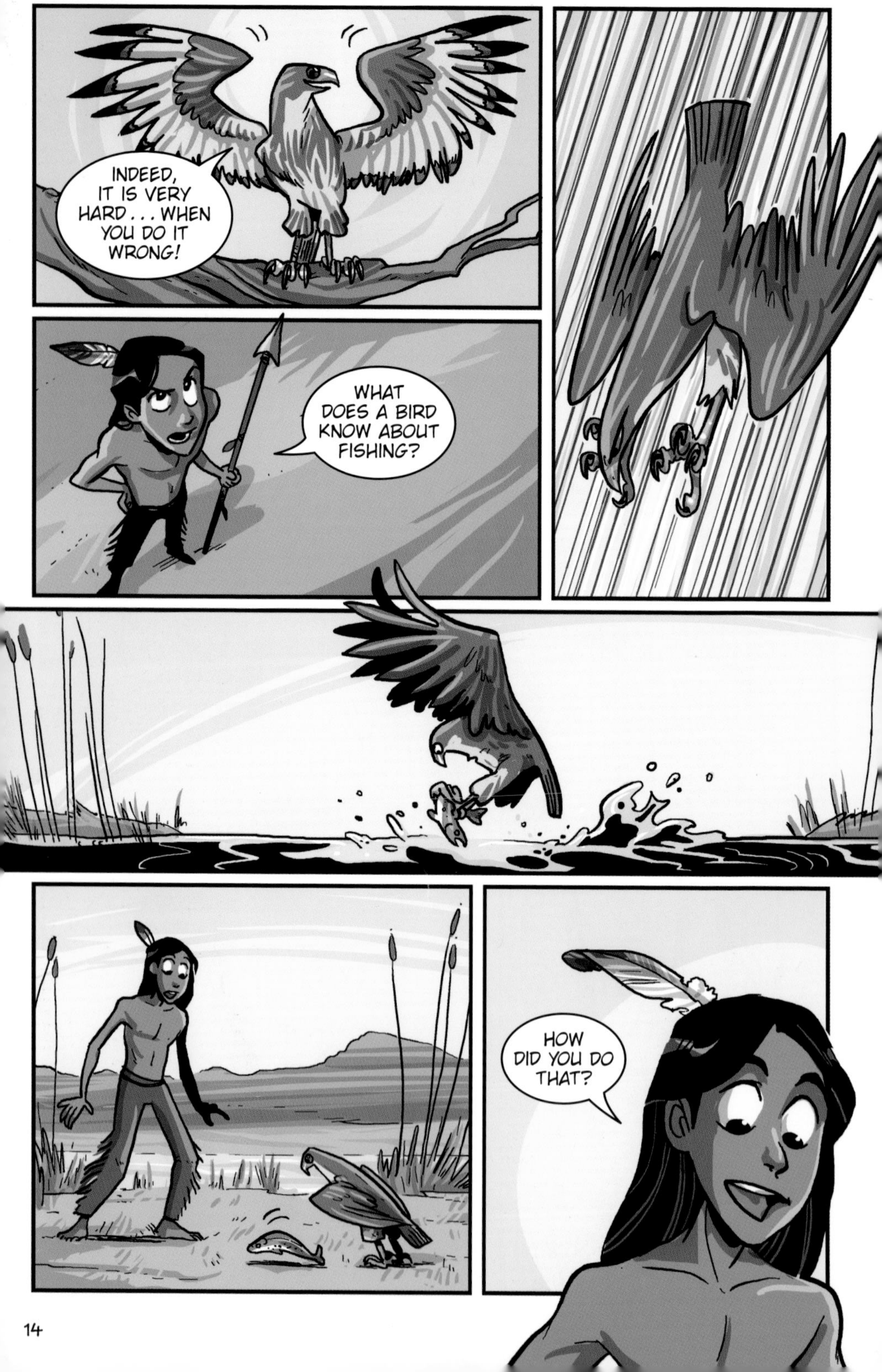
INDEED, IT IS VERY HARD . . . WHEN YOU DO IT WRONG!
WHAT DOES A BIRD KNOW ABOUT FISHING?
HOW DID YOU DO THAT?

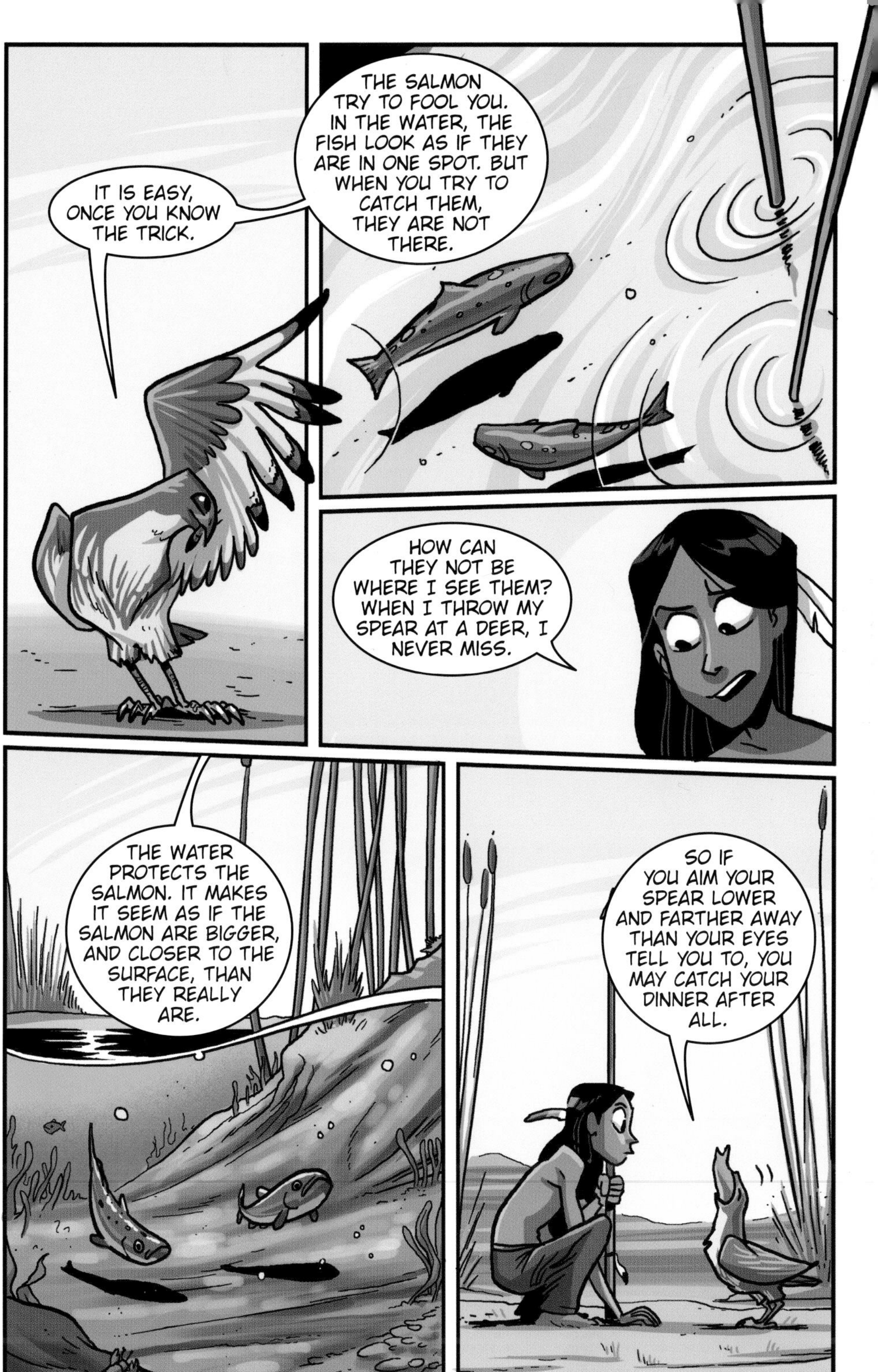
IT IS EASY, ONCE YOU KNOW THE TRICK.
THE SALMON TRY TO FOOL YOU. IN THE WATER, THE FISH LOOK AS IF THEY ARE IN ONE SPOT. BUT WHEN YOU TRY TO CATCH THEM, THEY ARE NOT THERE.
HOW CAN THEY NOT BE WHERE I SEE THEM? WHEN I THROW MY SPEAR AT A DEER, I NEVER MISS.
THE WATER PROTECTS THE SALMON. IT MAKES IT SEEM AS IF THE SALMON ARE BIGGER, AND CLOSER TO THE SURFACE, THAN THEY REALLY ARE.
SO IF YOU AIM YOUR SPEAR LOWER AND FARTHER AWAY THAN YOUR EYES TELL YOU TO, YOU MAY CATCH YOUR DINNER AFTER ALL.

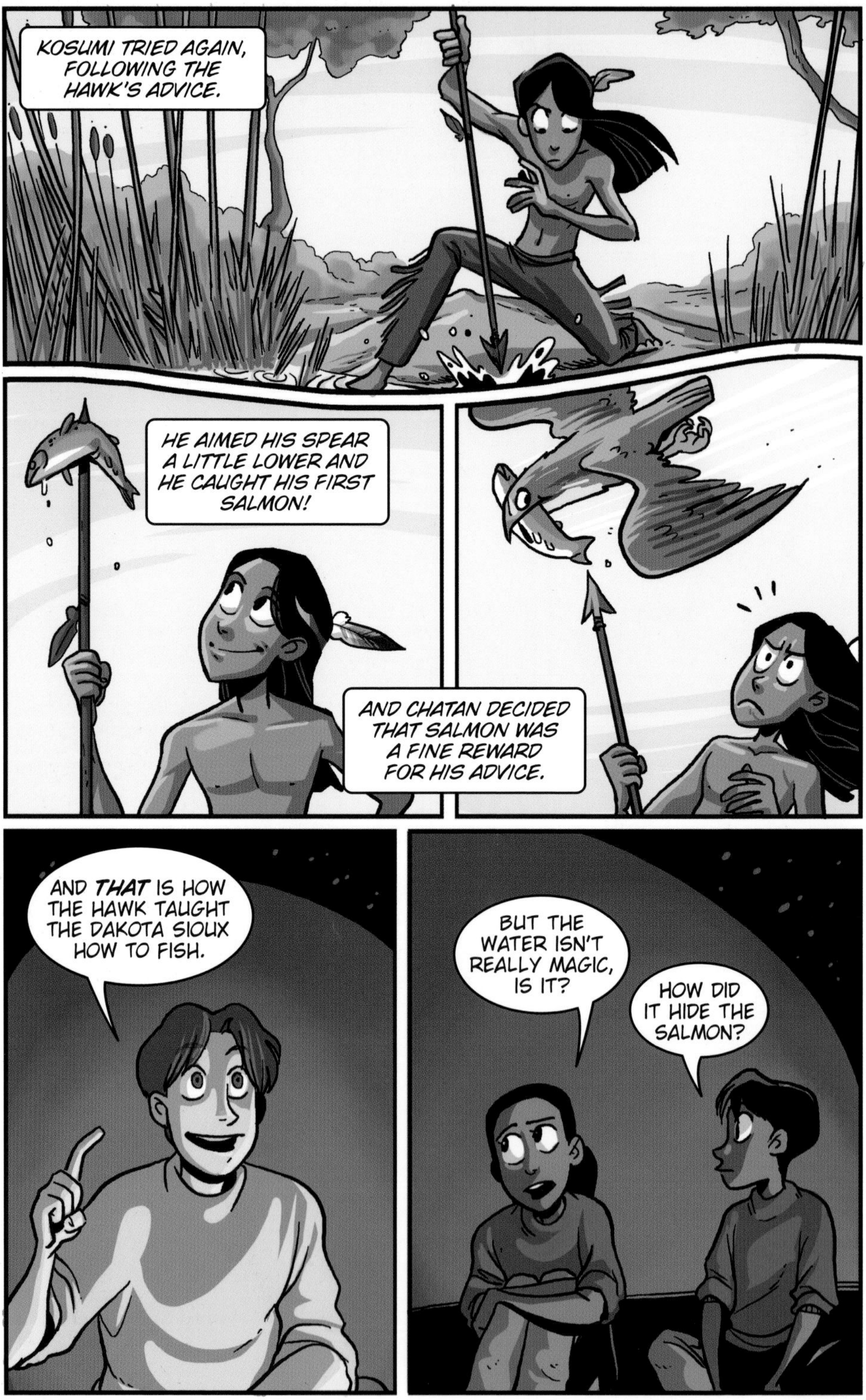
KOSUMI TRIED AGAIN, FOLLOWING THE HAWK'S ADVICE.
HE AIMED HIS SPEAR A LITTLE LOWER AND HE CAUGHT HIS FIRST SALMON!
AND CHATAN DECIDED THAT SALMON WAS A FINE REWARD FOR HIS ADVICE.
AND *THAT* IS HOW THE HAWK TAUGHT THE DAKOTA SIOUX HOW TO FISH.
BUT THE WATER ISN'T REALLY MAGIC, IS IT?
HOW DID IT HIDE THE SALMON?

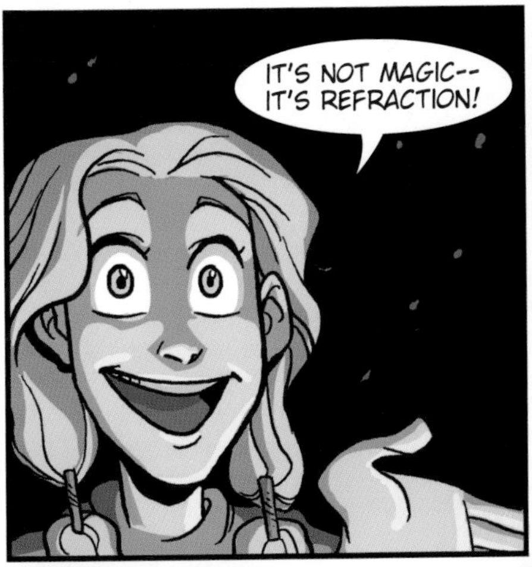
IT'S NOT MAGIC--
IT'S REFRACTION!

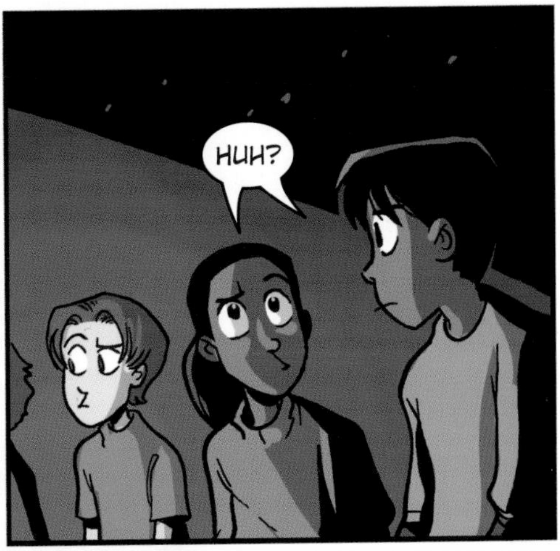
HUH?

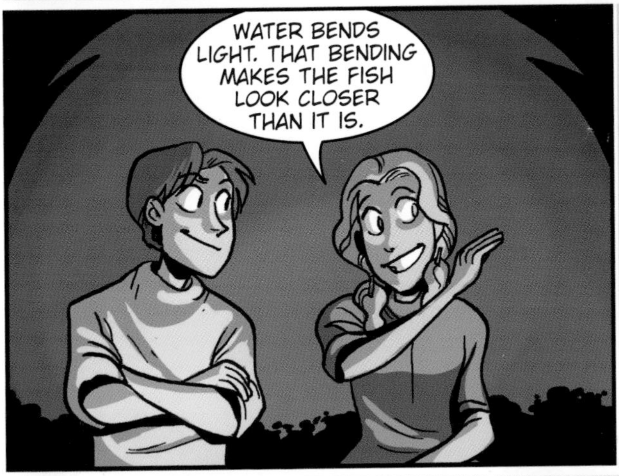
WATER BENDS LIGHT. THAT BENDING MAKES THE FISH LOOK CLOSER THAN IT IS.

Water is denser than air. When a wave of light enters water, it slows down. The change in speed also changes the light wave's direction, "bending" it. This makes underwater objects appear to be in a different location when viewed from above.

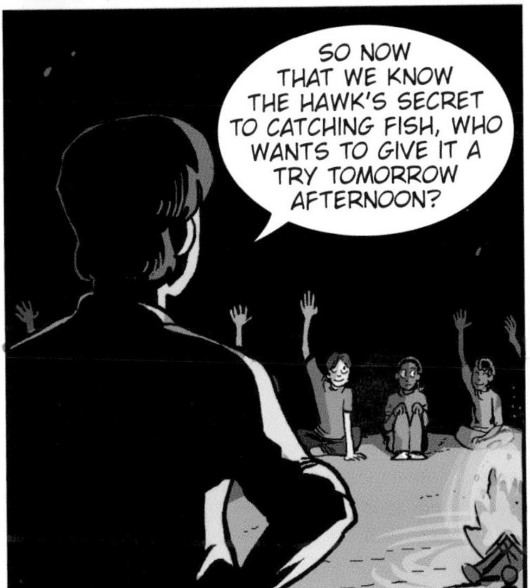
SO NOW THAT WE KNOW THE HAWK'S SECRET TO CATCHING FISH, WHO WANTS TO GIVE IT A TRY TOMORROW AFTERNOON?

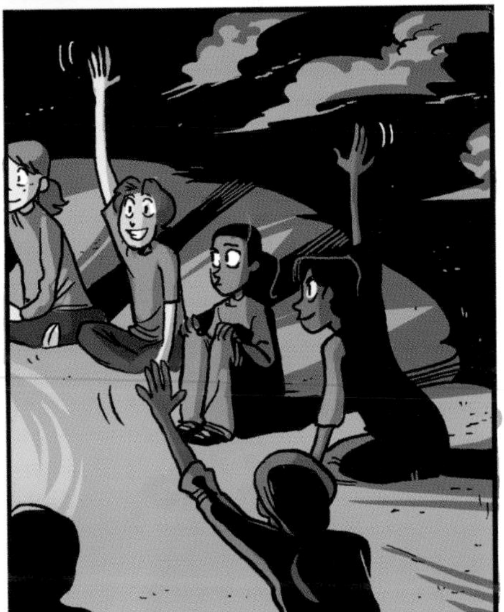

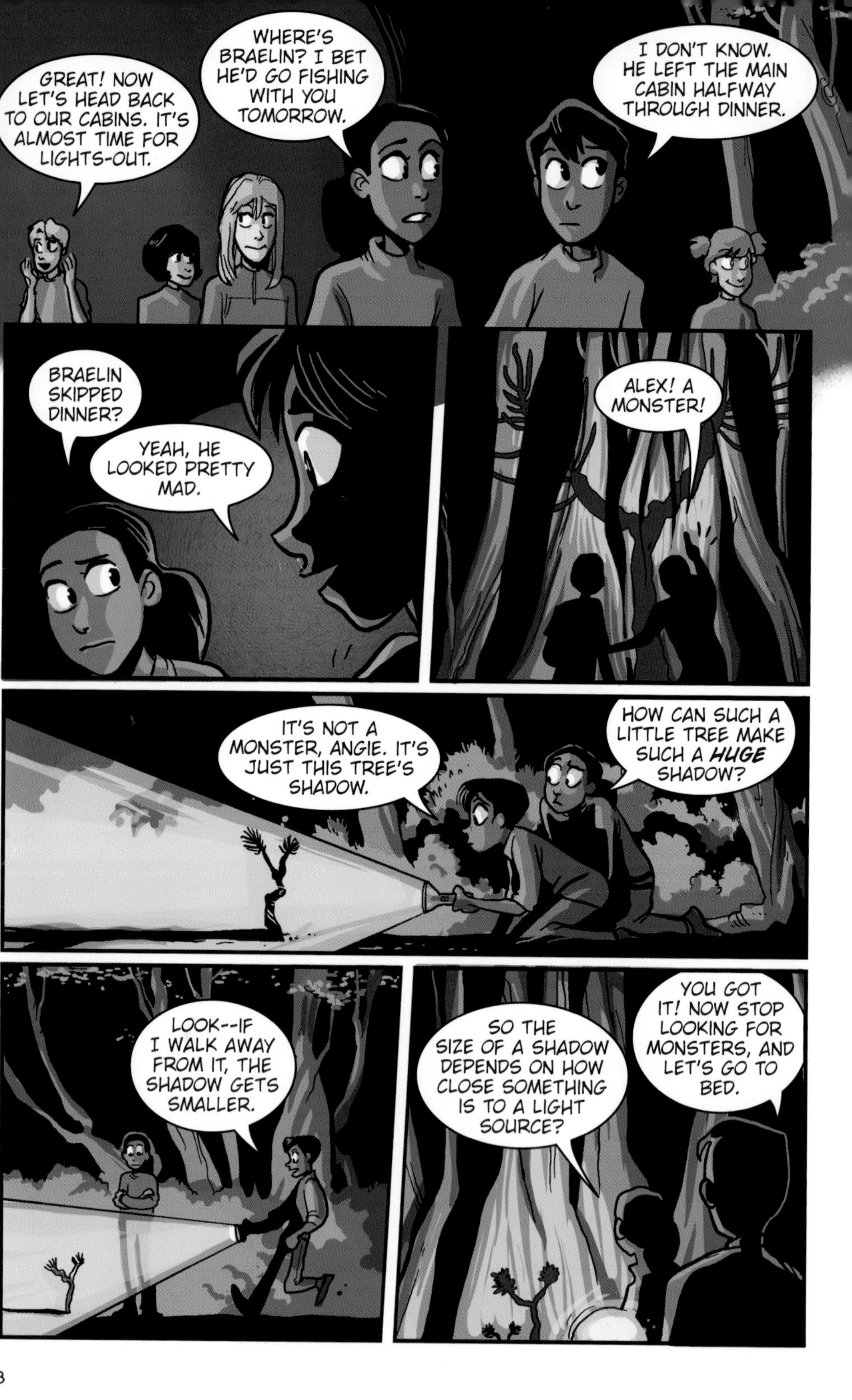
GREAT! NOW LET'S HEAD BACK TO OUR CABINS. IT'S ALMOST TIME FOR LIGHTS-OUT.
WHERE'S BRAELIN? I BET HE'D GO FISHING WITH YOU TOMORROW.
I DON'T KNOW. HE LEFT THE MAIN CABIN HALFWAY THROUGH DINNER.
BRAELIN SKIPPED DINNER?
YEAH, HE LOOKED PRETTY MAD.
ALEX! A MONSTER!
IT'S NOT A MONSTER, ANGIE. IT'S JUST THIS TREE'S SHADOW.
HOW CAN SUCH A LITTLE TREE MAKE SUCH A *HUGE* SHADOW?
LOOK--IF I WALK AWAY FROM IT, THE SHADOW GETS SMALLER.
SO THE SIZE OF A SHADOW DEPENDS ON HOW CLOSE SOMETHING IS TO A LIGHT SOURCE?
YOU GOT IT! NOW STOP LOOKING FOR MONSTERS, AND LET'S GO TO BED.

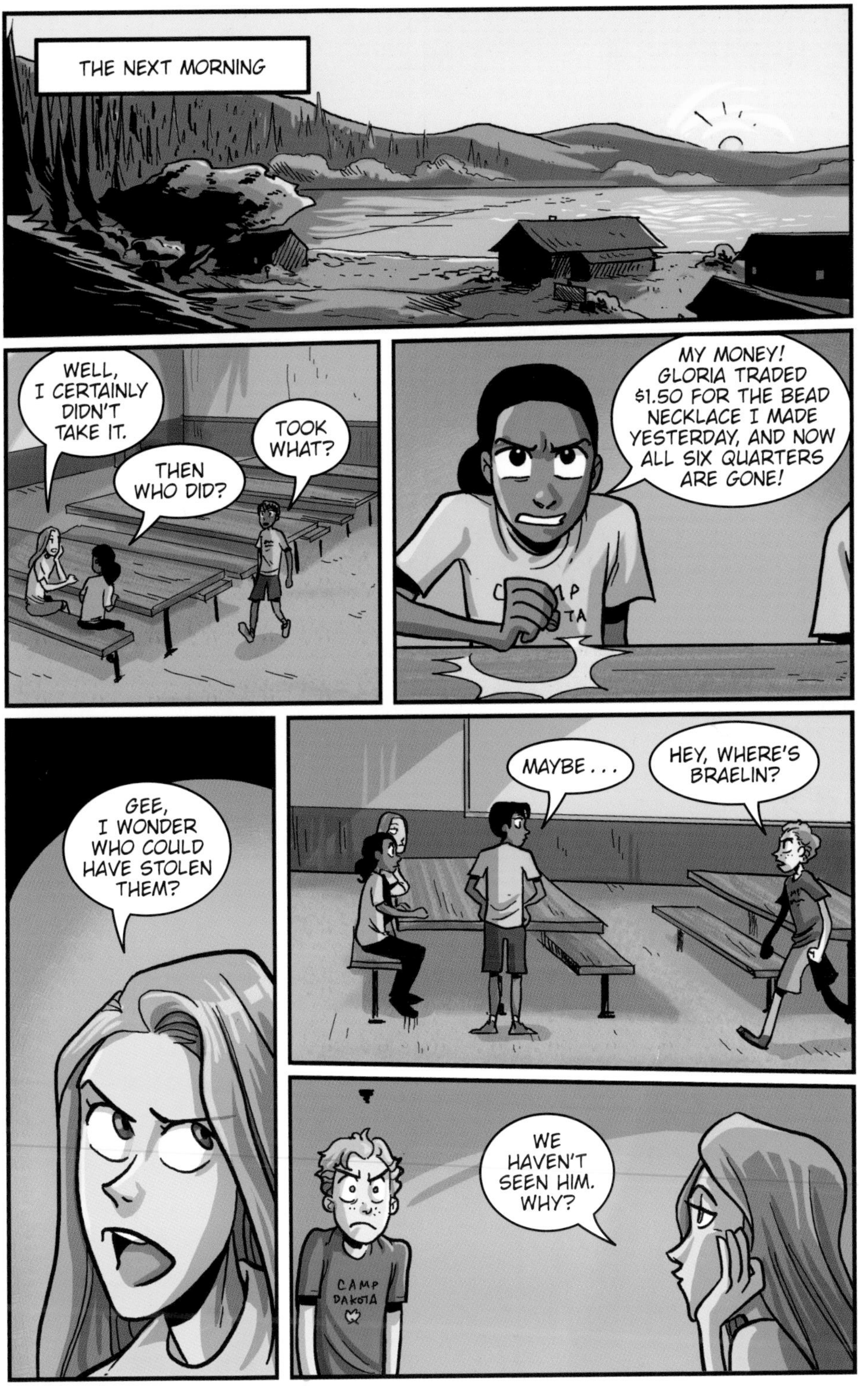
THE NEXT MORNING
WELL, I CERTAINLY DIDN'T TAKE IT.
THEN WHO DID?
TOOK WHAT?
MY MONEY! GLORIA TRADED $1.50 FOR THE BEAD NECKLACE I MADE YESTERDAY, AND NOW ALL SIX QUARTERS ARE GONE!
GEE, I WONDER WHO COULD HAVE STOLEN THEM?
MAYBE . . .
HEY, WHERE'S BRAELIN?
WE HAVEN'T SEEN HIM. WHY?
CAMP DAKOTA

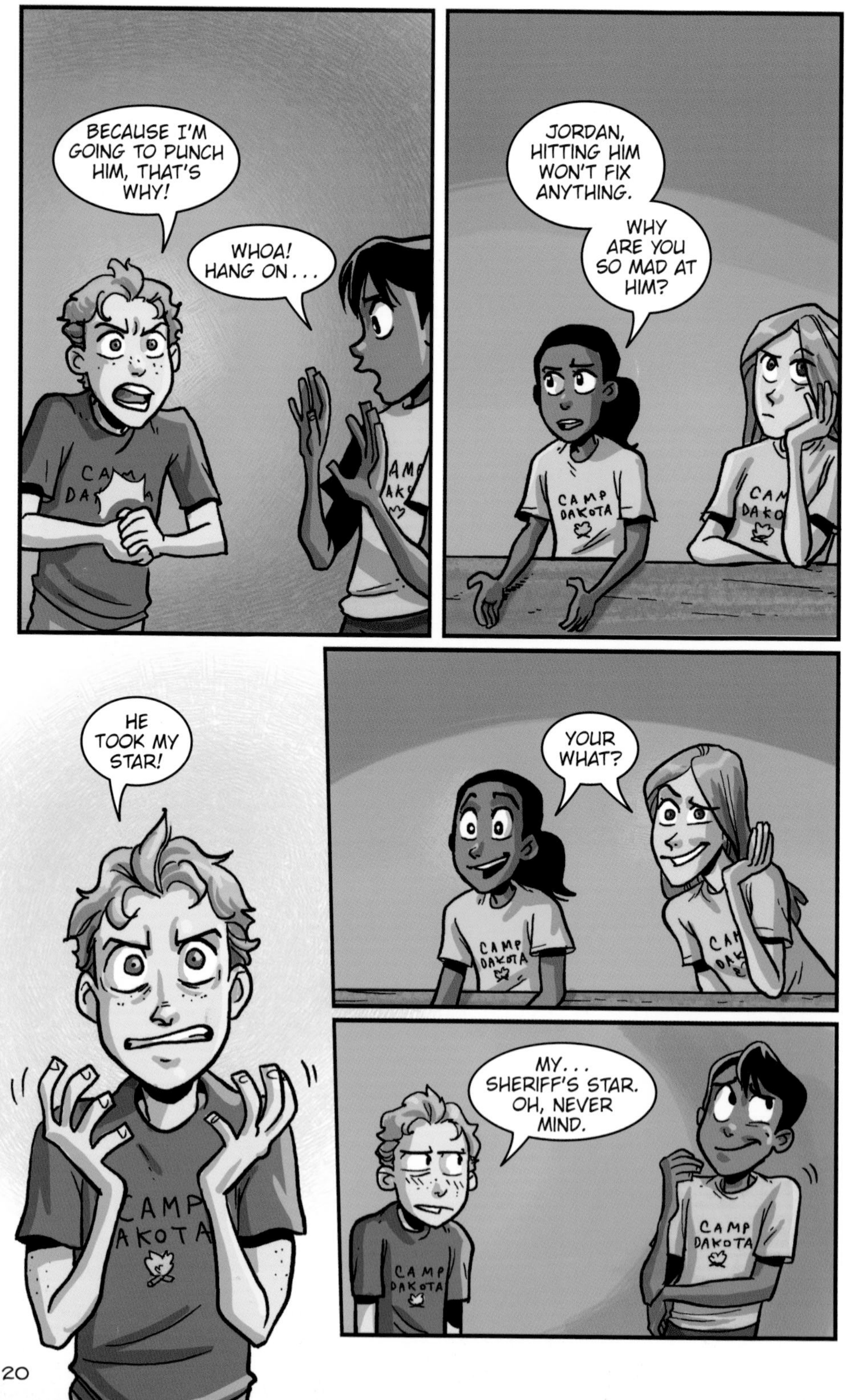
BECAUSE I'M GOING TO PUNCH HIM, THAT'S WHY!
WHOA! HANG ON . . .
JORDAN, HITTING HIM WON'T FIX ANYTHING.
WHY ARE YOU SO MAD AT HIM?
HE TOOK MY STAR!
YOUR WHAT?
MY . . . SHERIFF'S STAR. OH, NEVER MIND.

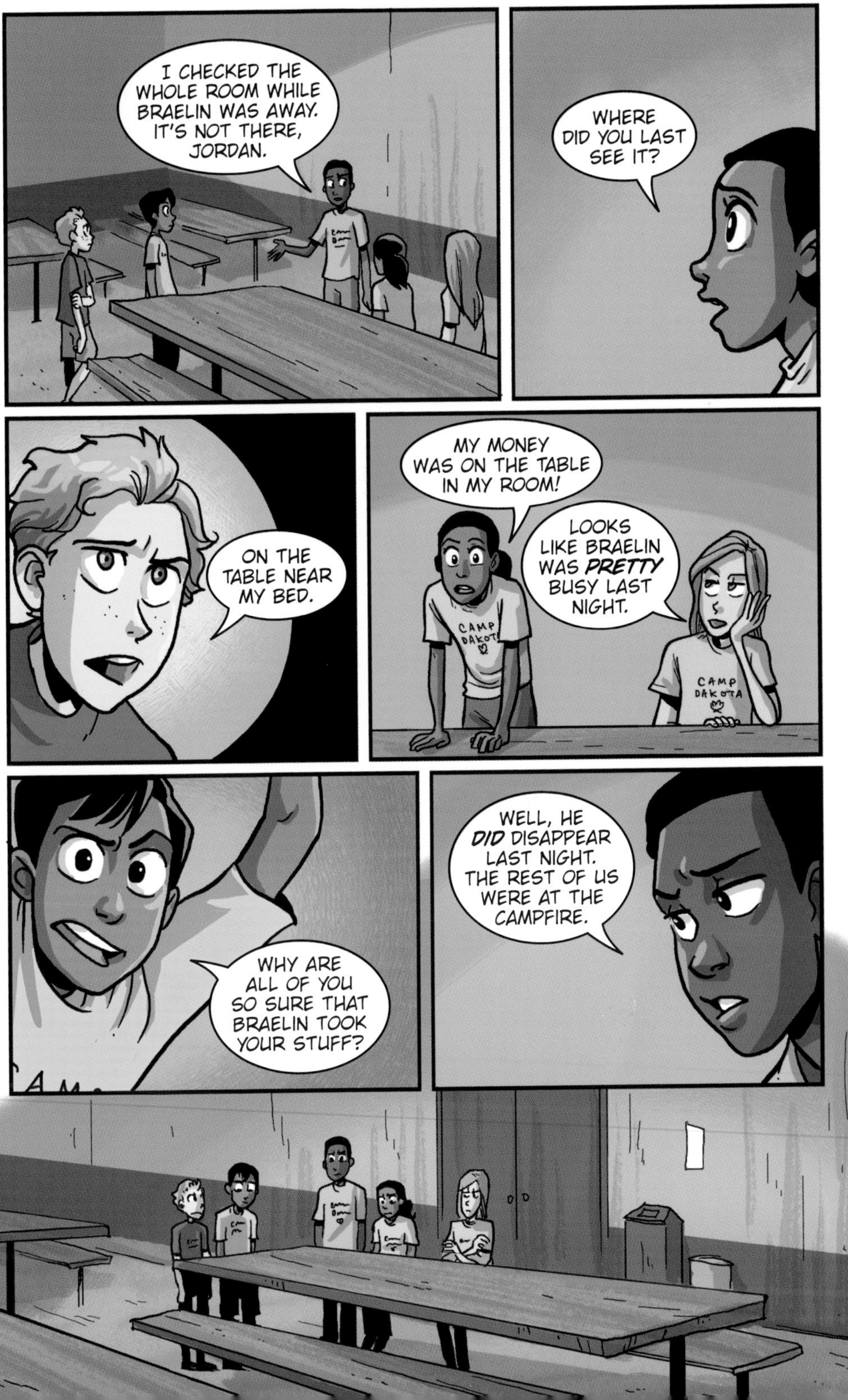
I CHECKED THE WHOLE ROOM WHILE BRAELIN WAS AWAY. IT'S NOT THERE, JORDAN.
WHERE DID YOU LAST SEE IT?
ON THE TABLE NEAR MY BED.
MY MONEY WAS ON THE TABLE IN MY ROOM!
LOOKS LIKE BRAELIN WAS PRETTY BUSY LAST NIGHT.
CAMP DAKOTA
CAMP DAKOTA
WHY ARE ALL OF YOU SO SURE THAT BRAELIN TOOK YOUR STUFF?
WELL, HE DID DISAPPEAR LAST NIGHT. THE REST OF US WERE AT THE CAMPFIRE.

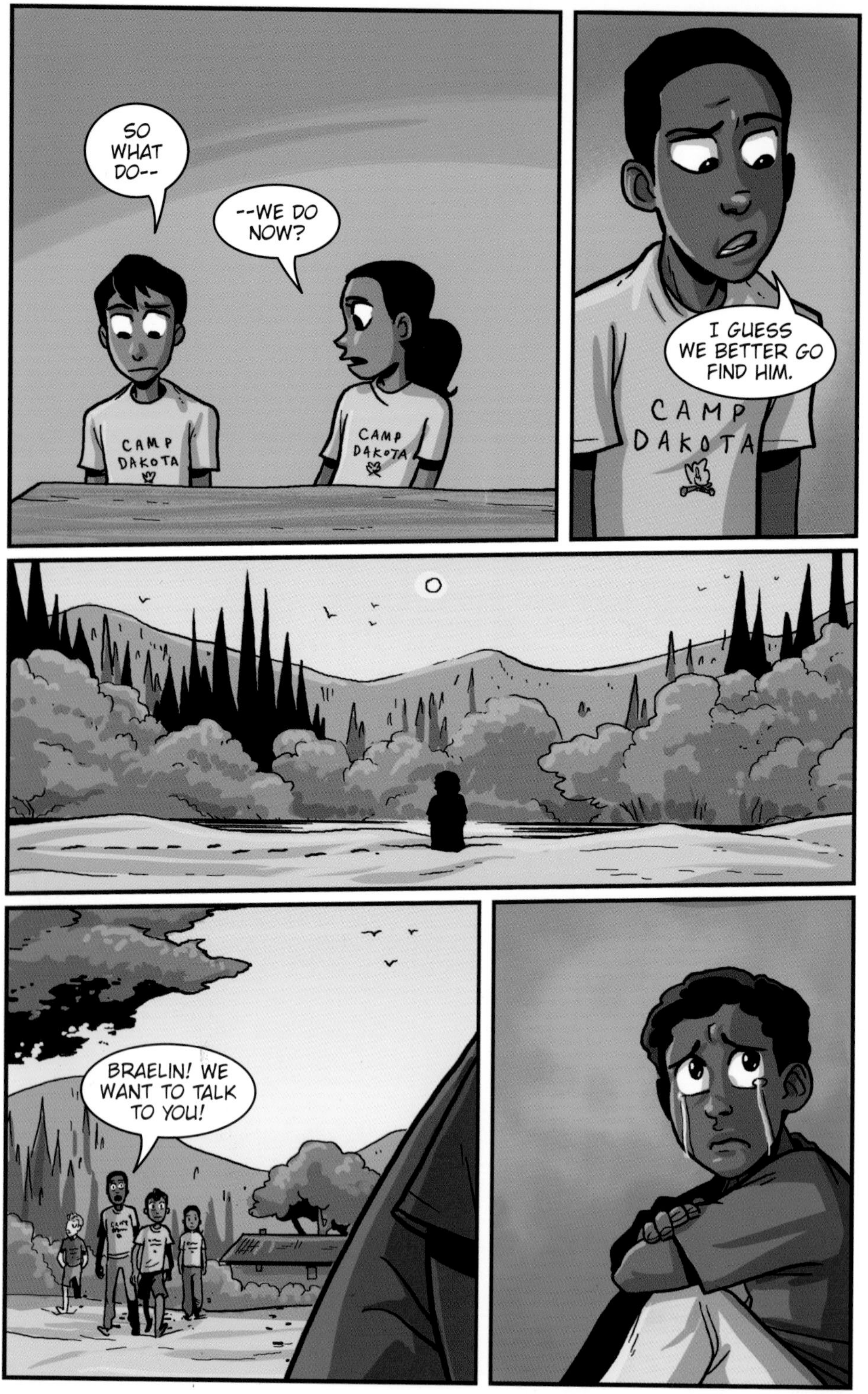
SO WHAT DO--
--WE DO NOW?
CAMP DAKOTA
CAMP DAKOTA
I GUESS WE BETTER GO FIND HIM.
CAMP DAKOTA
BRAELIN! WE WANT TO TALK TO YOU!

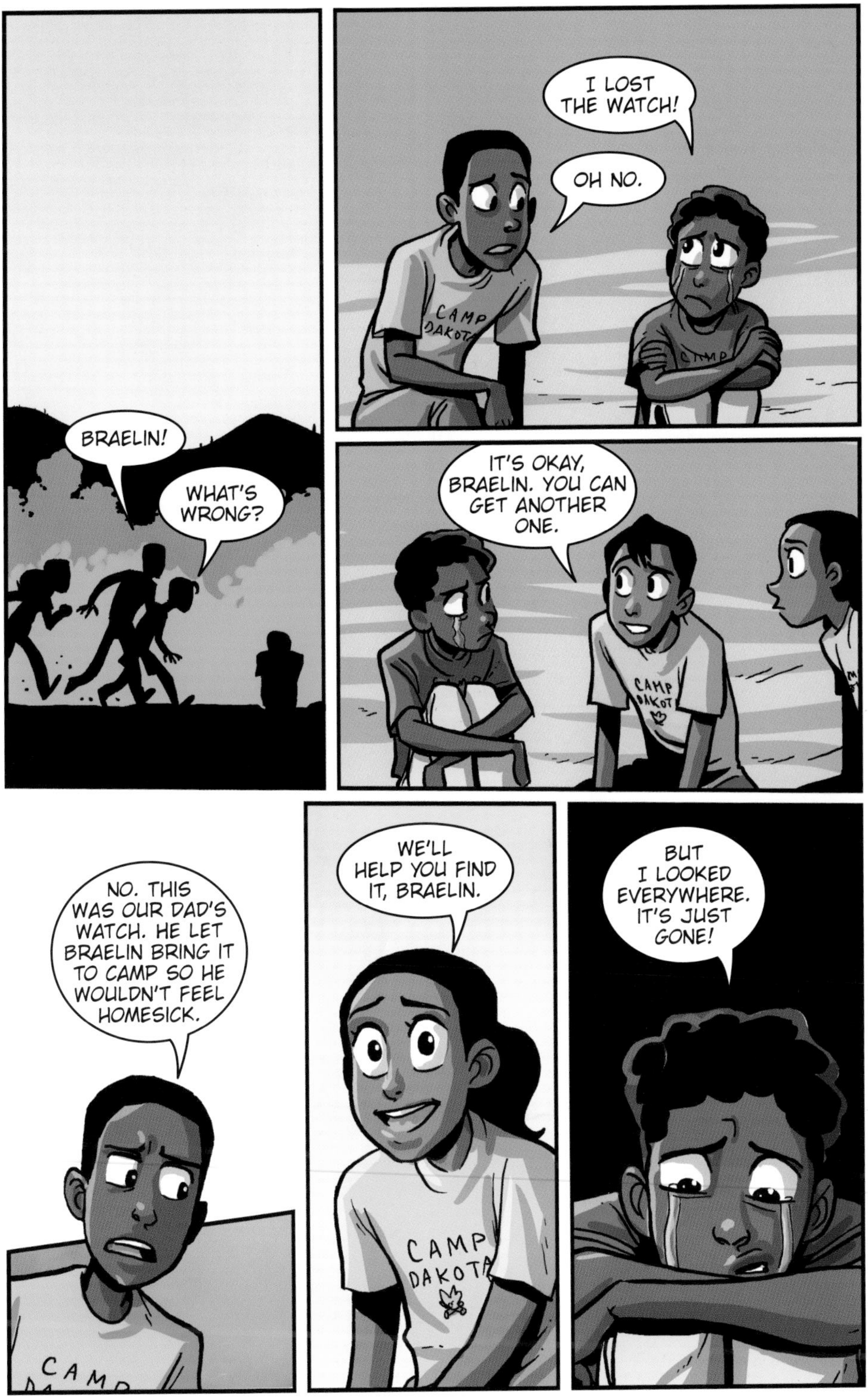
BRAELIN!
WHAT'S WRONG?
I LOST THE WATCH!
OH NO.
IT'S OKAY, BRAELIN. YOU CAN GET ANOTHER ONE.
NO. THIS WAS OUR DAD'S WATCH. HE LET BRAELIN BRING IT TO CAMP SO HE WOULDN'T FEEL HOMESICK.
WE'LL HELP YOU FIND IT, BRAELIN.
BUT I LOOKED EVERYWHERE. IT'S JUST GONE!

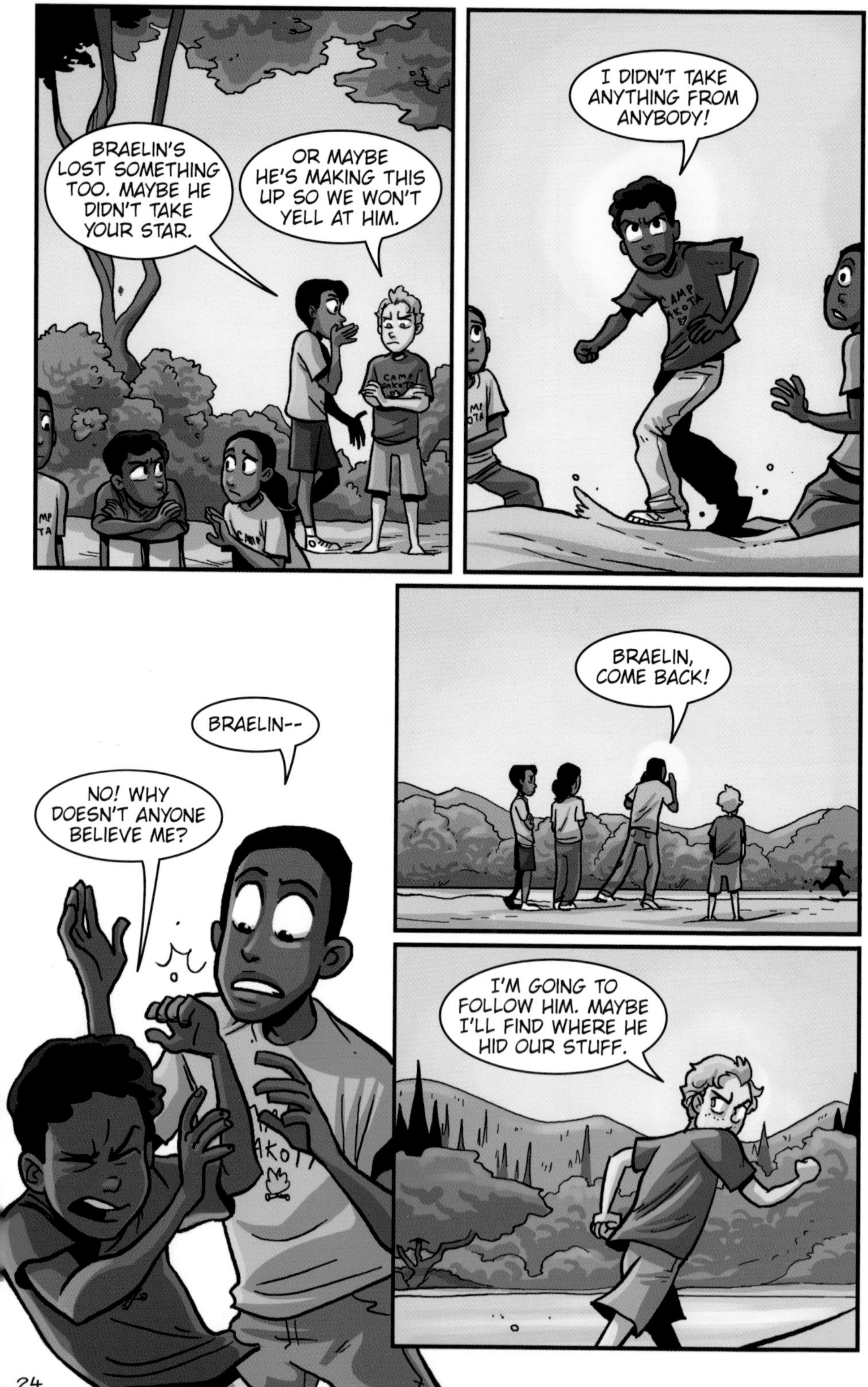
BRAELIN'S LOST SOMETHING TOO. MAYBE HE DIDN'T TAKE YOUR STAR.
OR MAYBE HE'S MAKING THIS UP SO WE WON'T YELL AT HIM.
I DIDN'T TAKE ANYTHING FROM ANYBODY!
BRAELIN--
NO! WHY DOESN'T ANYONE BELIEVE ME?
BRAELIN, COME BACK!
I'M GOING TO FOLLOW HIM. MAYBE I'LL FIND WHERE HE HID OUR STUFF.

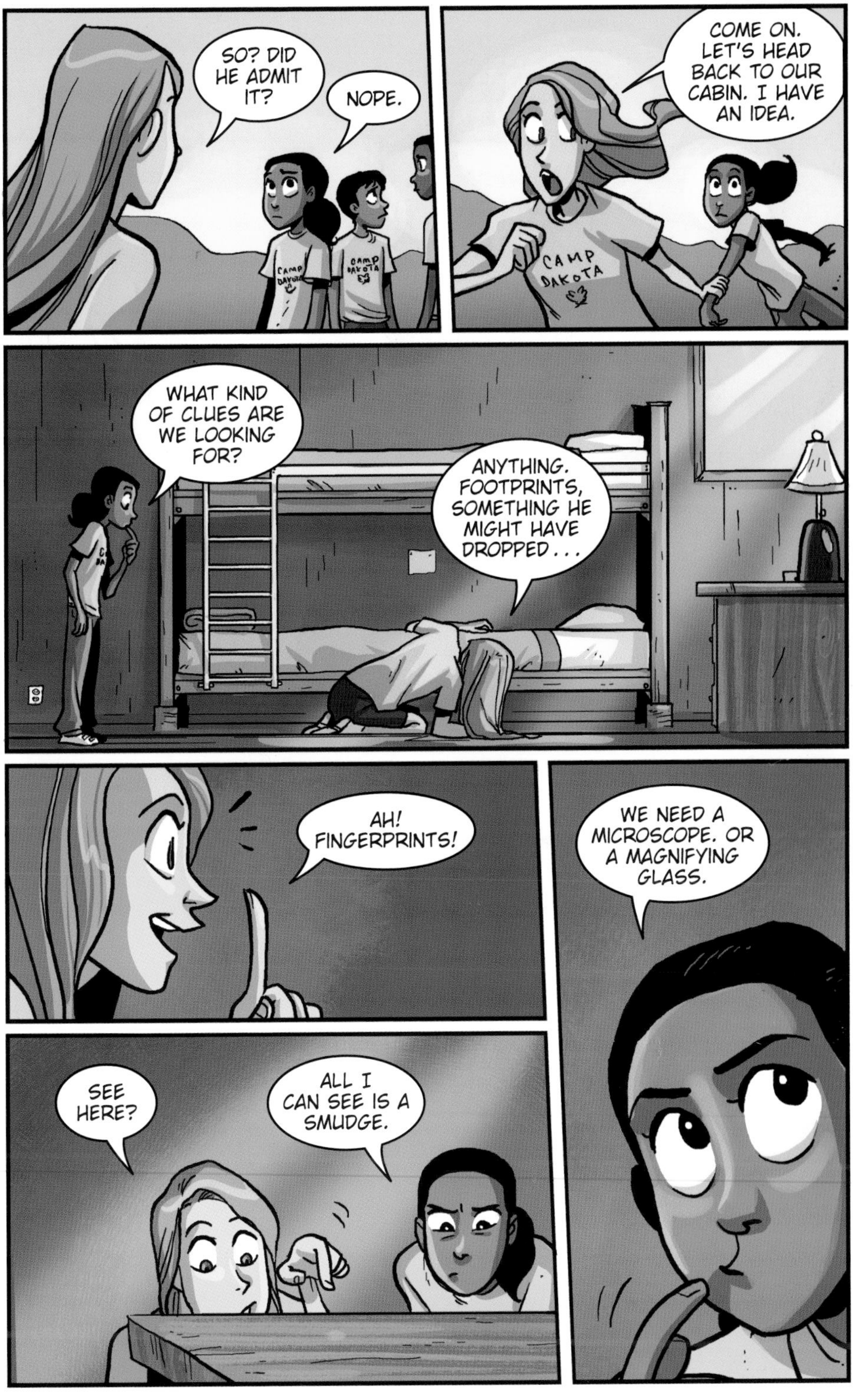
SO? DID HE ADMIT IT?
NOPE.
COME ON. LET'S HEAD BACK TO OUR CABIN. I HAVE AN IDEA.
CAMP DAKOTA
WHAT KIND OF CLUES ARE WE LOOKING FOR?
ANYTHING. FOOTPRINTS, SOMETHING HE MIGHT HAVE DROPPED . . .
AH! FINGERPRINTS!
WE NEED A MICROSCOPE. OR A MAGNIFYING GLASS.
SEE HERE?
ALL I CAN SEE IS A SMUDGE.

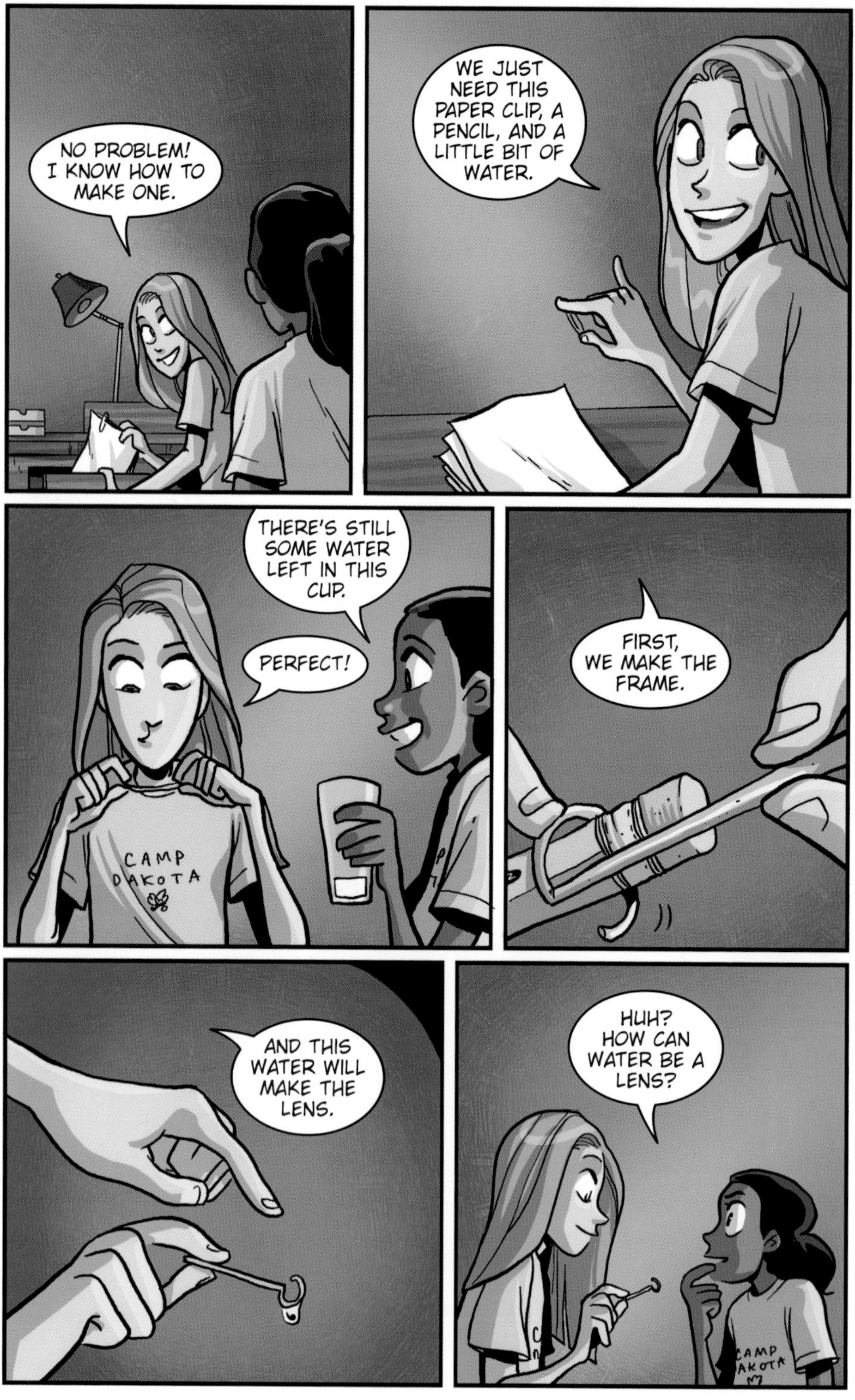
NO PROBLEM! I KNOW HOW TO MAKE ONE.
WE JUST NEED THIS PAPER CLIP, A PENCIL, AND A LITTLE BIT OF WATER.
THERE'S STILL SOME WATER LEFT IN THIS CUP.
PERFECT!
CAMP DAKOTA
FIRST, WE MAKE THE FRAME.
AND THIS WATER WILL MAKE THE LENS.
HUH? HOW CAN WATER BE A LENS?
CAMP DAKOTA

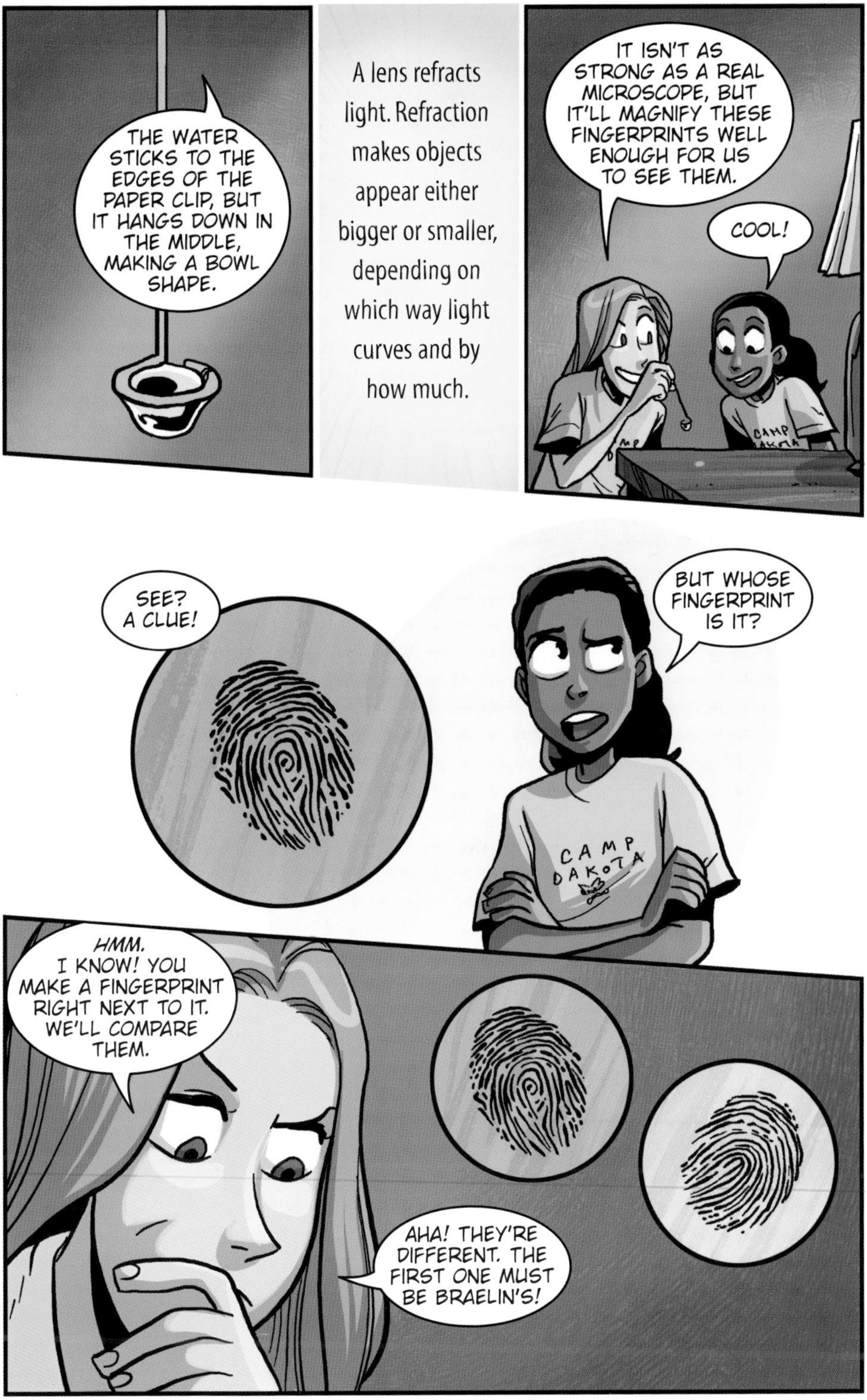
THE WATER STICKS TO THE EDGES OF THE PAPER CLIP, BUT IT HANGS DOWN IN THE MIDDLE, MAKING A BOWL SHAPE.
A lens refracts light. Refraction makes objects appear either bigger or smaller, depending on which way light curves and by how much.
IT ISN'T AS STRONG AS A REAL MICROSCOPE, BUT IT'LL MAGNIFY THESE FINGERPRINTS WELL ENOUGH FOR US TO SEE THEM.
COOL!
SEE? A CLUE!
BUT WHOSE FINGERPRINT IS IT?
CAMP DAKOTA
HMM. I KNOW! YOU MAKE A FINGERPRINT RIGHT NEXT TO IT. WE'LL COMPARE THEM.
AHA! THEY'RE DIFFERENT. THE FIRST ONE MUST BE BRAELIN'S!

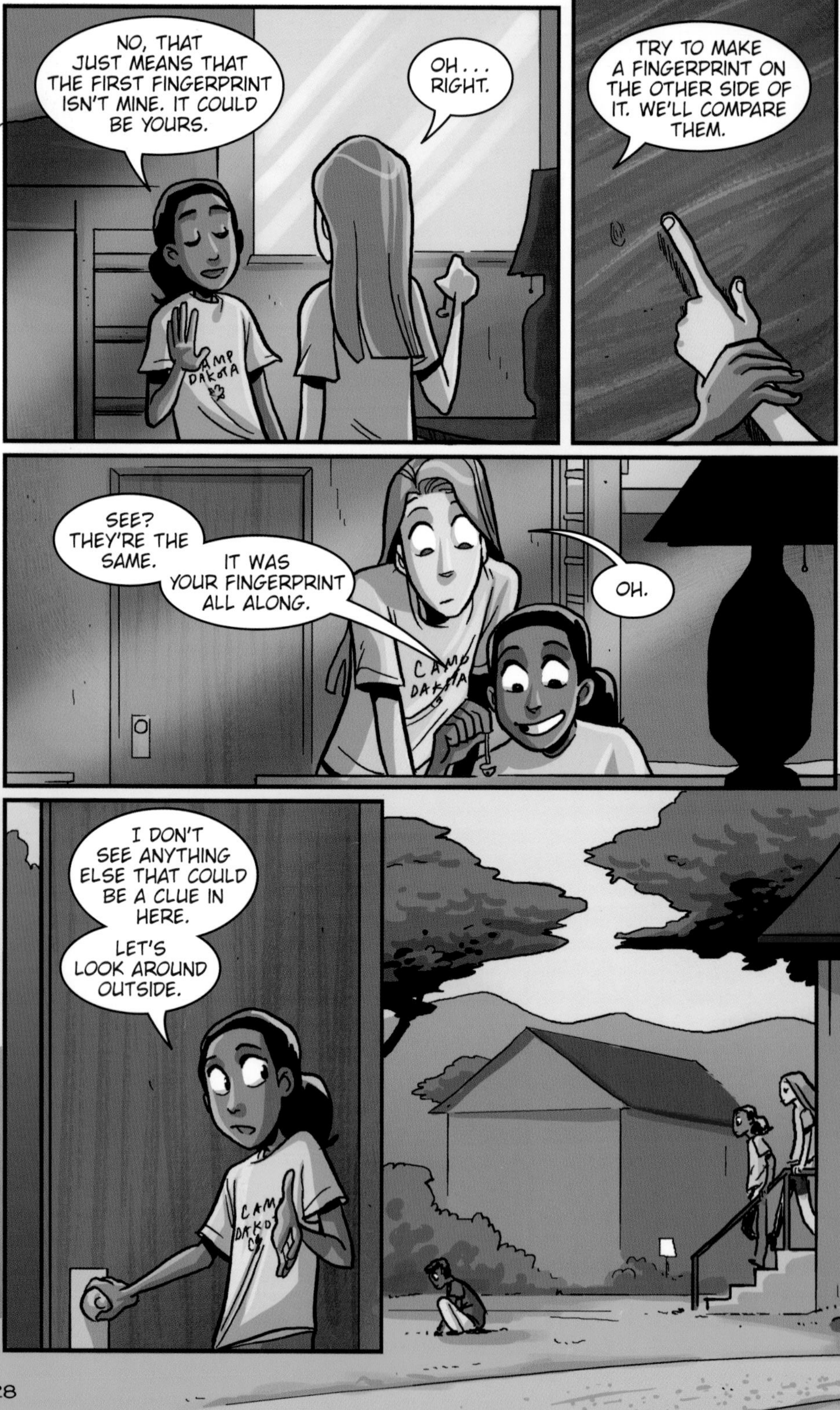
NO, THAT JUST MEANS THAT THE FIRST FINGERPRINT ISN'T MINE. IT COULD BE YOURS.
OH . . . RIGHT.
TRY TO MAKE A FINGERPRINT ON THE OTHER SIDE OF IT. WE'LL COMPARE THEM.
SEE? THEY'RE THE SAME.
IT WAS YOUR FINGERPRINT ALL ALONG.
OH.
I DON'T SEE ANYTHING ELSE THAT COULD BE A CLUE IN HERE.
LET'S LOOK AROUND OUTSIDE.

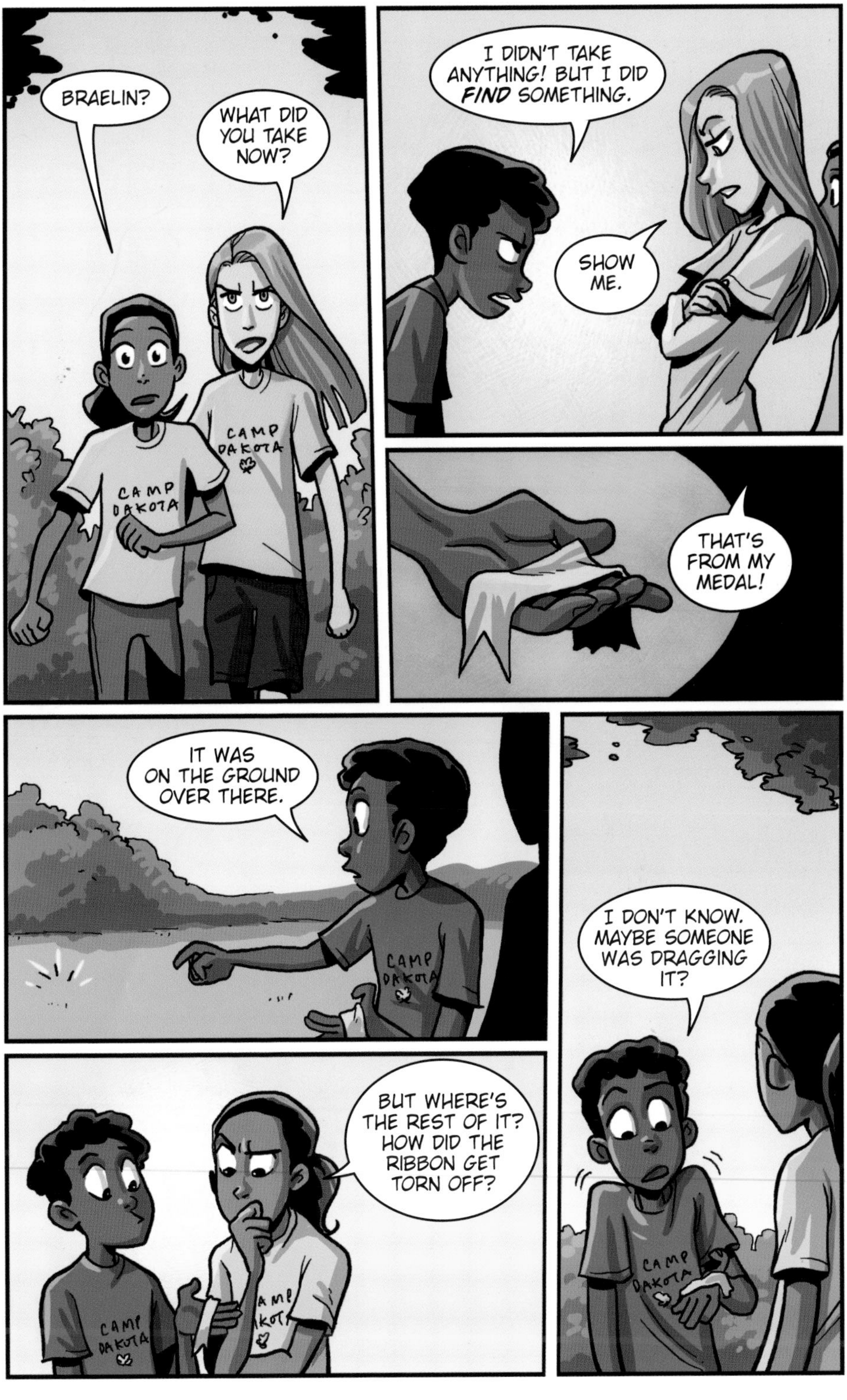
BRAELIN?
WHAT DID YOU TAKE NOW?
I DIDN'T TAKE ANYTHING! BUT I DID *FIND* SOMETHING.
SHOW ME.
THAT'S FROM MY MEDAL!
IT WAS ON THE GROUND OVER THERE.
BUT WHERE'S THE REST OF IT? HOW DID THE RIBBON GET TORN OFF?
I DON'T KNOW. MAYBE SOMEONE WAS DRAGGING IT?
CAMP DAKOTA

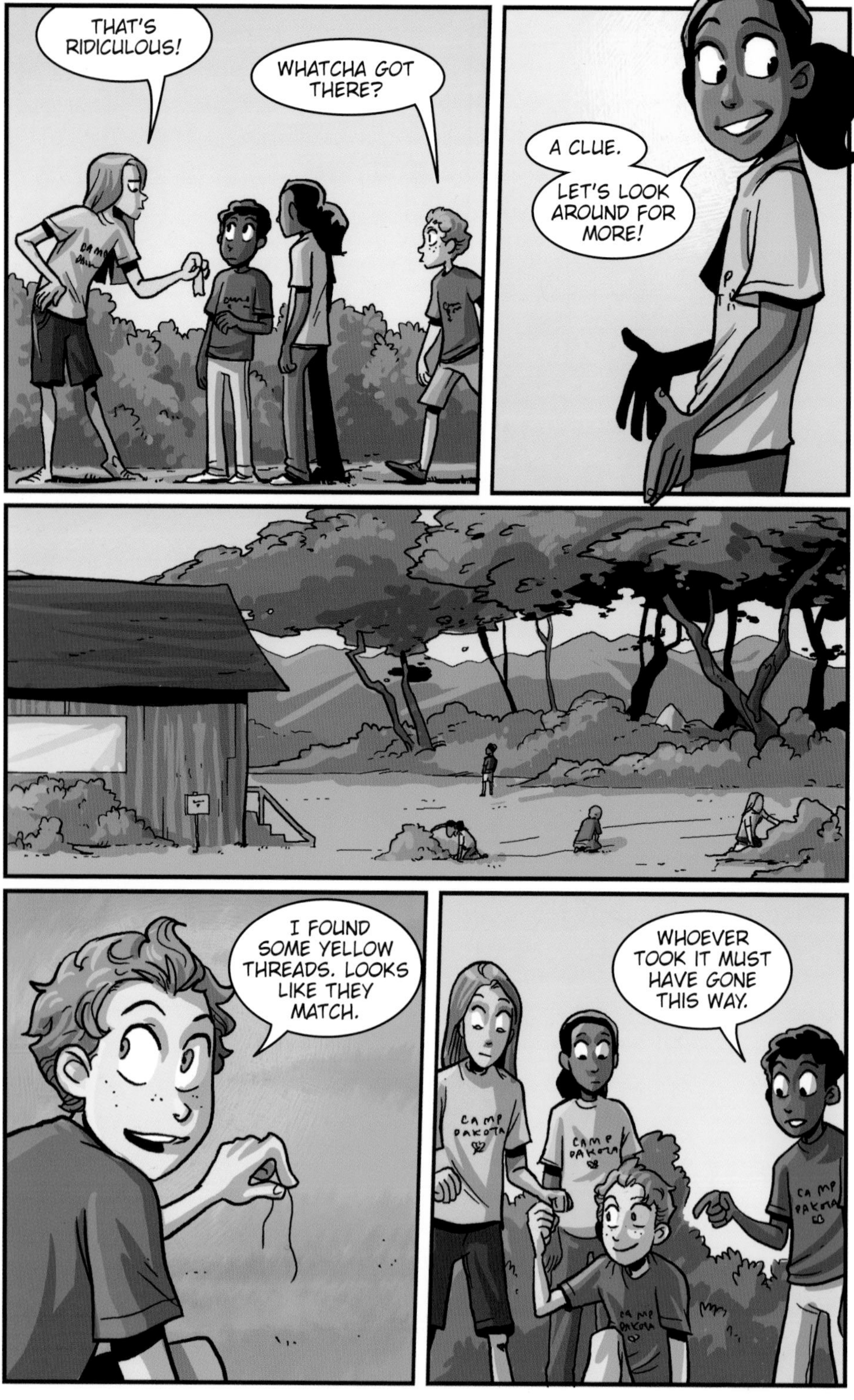
THAT'S RIDICULOUS!
WHATCHA GOT THERE?
A CLUE.
LET'S LOOK AROUND FOR MORE!
I FOUND SOME YELLOW THREADS. LOOKS LIKE THEY MATCH.
WHOEVER TOOK IT MUST HAVE GONE THIS WAY.

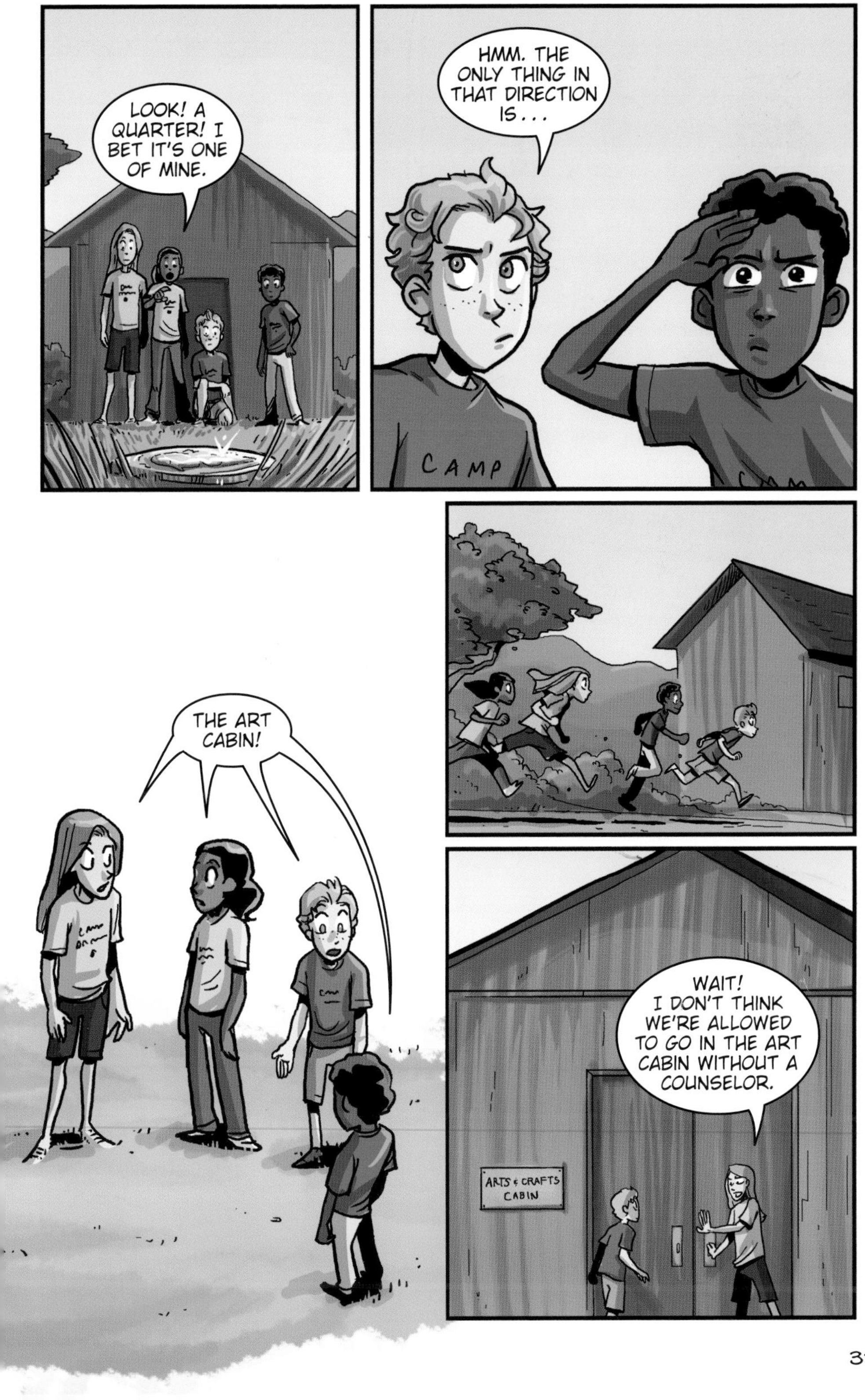
LOOK! A QUARTER! I BET IT'S ONE OF MINE.
HMM. THE ONLY THING IN THAT DIRECTION IS . . .
CAMP
THE ART CABIN!
WAIT! I DON'T THINK WE'RE ALLOWED TO GO IN THE ART CABIN WITHOUT A COUNSELOR.
ARTS & CRAFTS CABIN

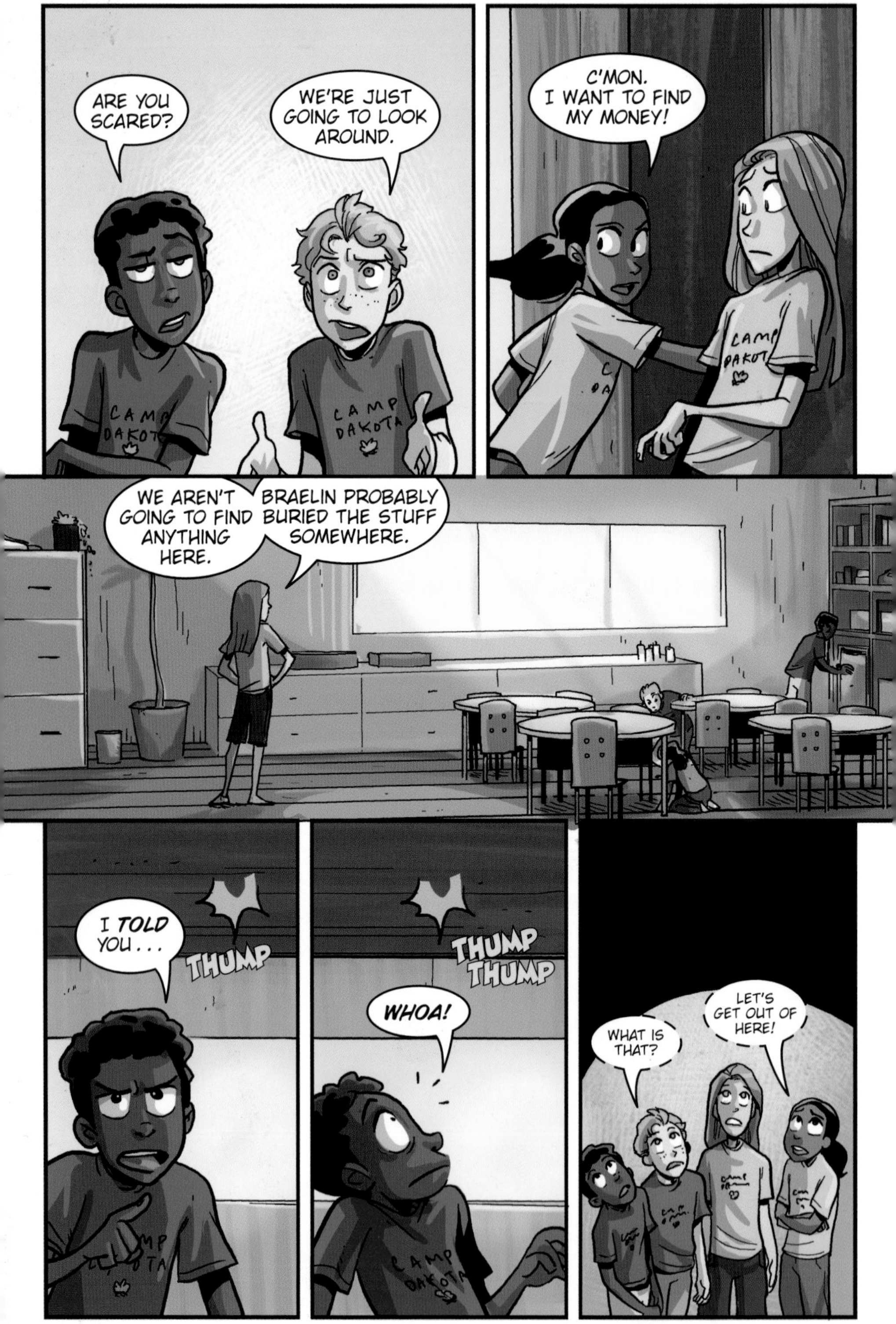

ARE YOU SCARED?
WE'RE JUST GOING TO LOOK AROUND.
C'MON. I WANT TO FIND MY MONEY!
CAMP DAKOTA
WE AREN'T GOING TO FIND ANYTHING HERE.
BRAELIN PROBABLY BURIED THE STUFF SOMEWHERE.
I TOLD YOU . . .
THUMP
THUMP THUMP
WHOA!
WHAT IS THAT?
LET'S GET OUT OF HERE!

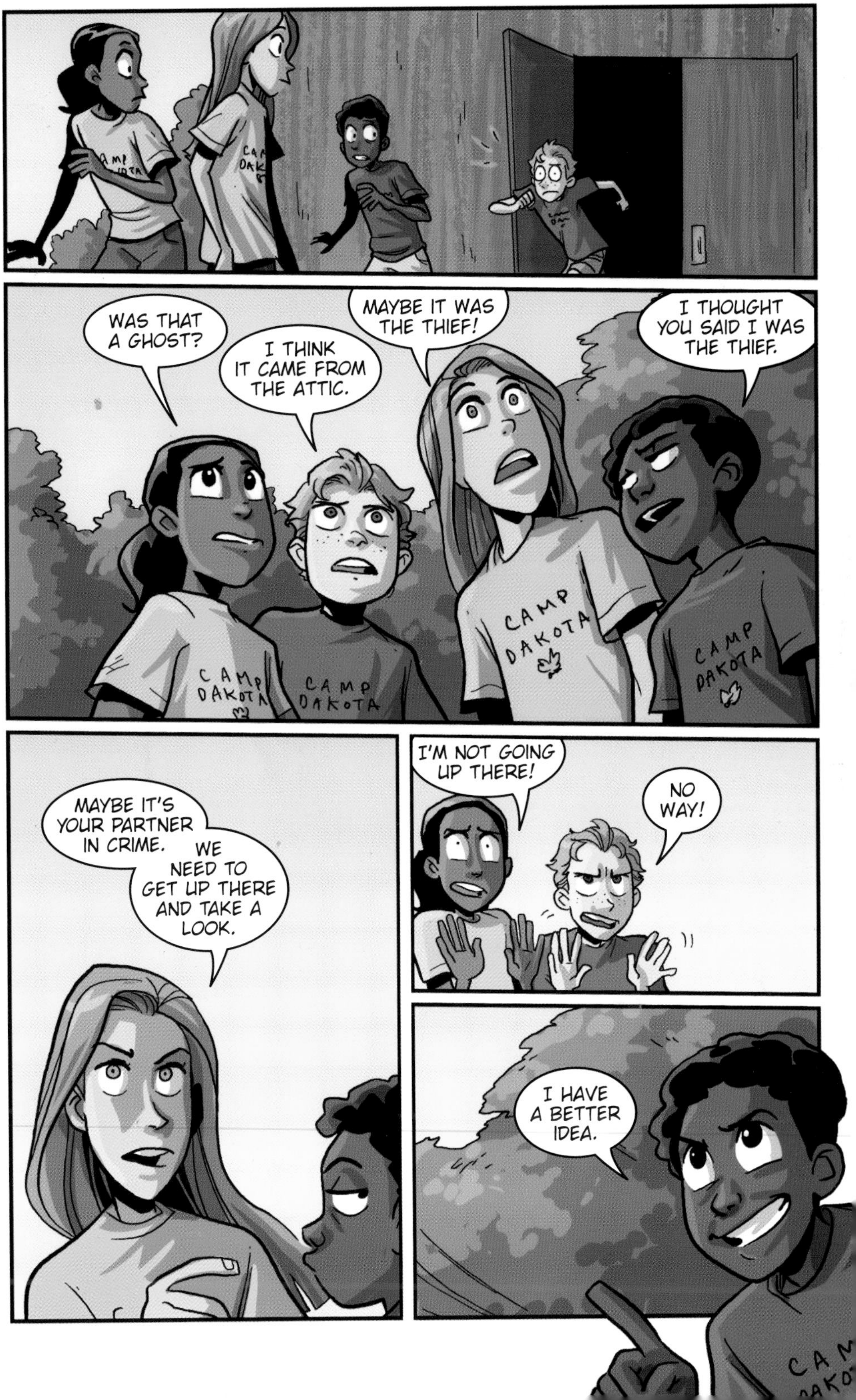

WAS THAT A GHOST?
I THINK IT CAME FROM THE ATTIC.
MAYBE IT WAS THE THIEF!
I THOUGHT YOU SAID I WAS THE THIEF.
MAYBE IT'S YOUR PARTNER IN CRIME.
WE NEED TO GET UP THERE AND TAKE A LOOK.
I'M NOT GOING UP THERE!
NO WAY!
I HAVE A BETTER IDEA.

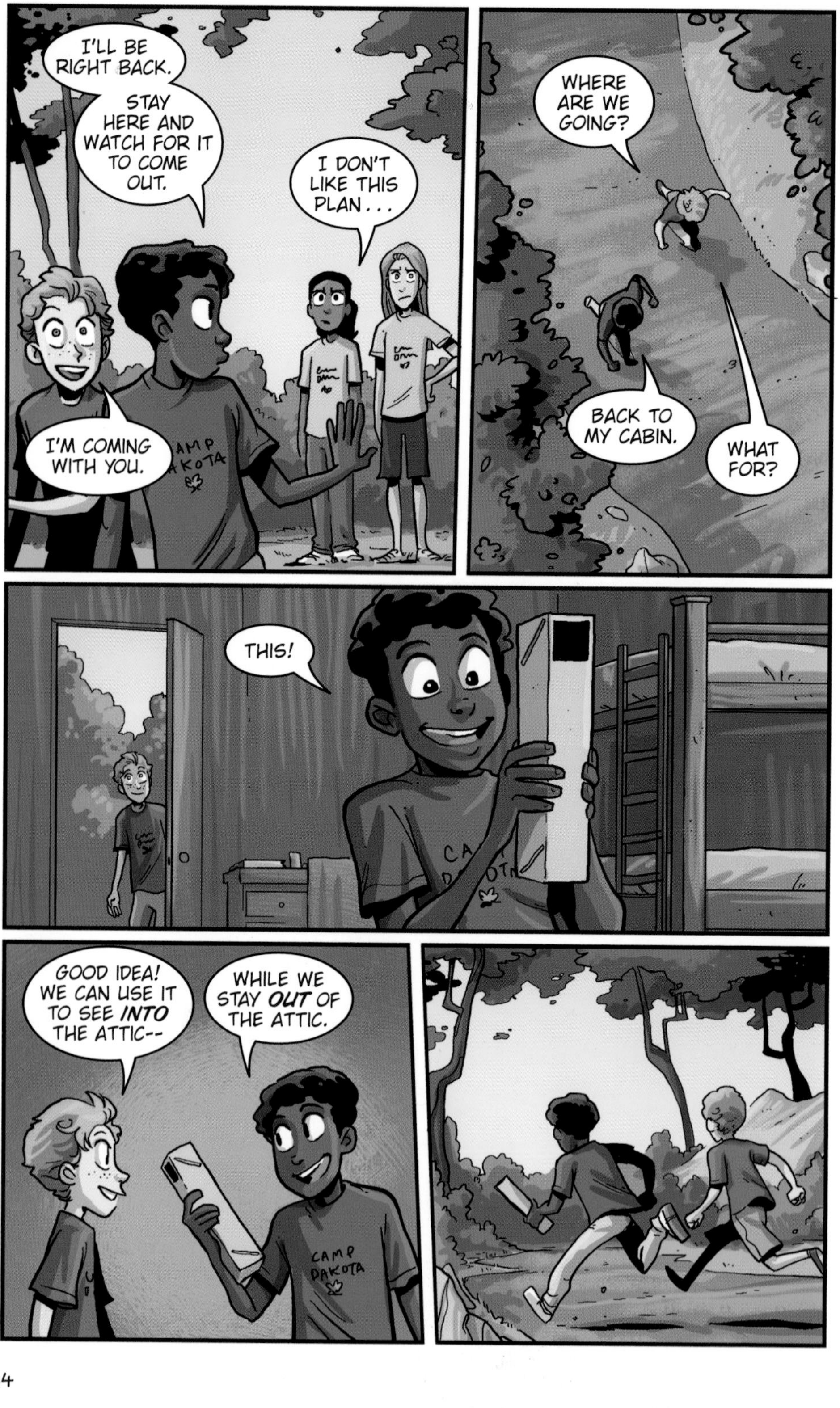
I'LL BE RIGHT BACK.
STAY HERE AND WATCH FOR IT TO COME OUT.
I DON'T LIKE THIS PLAN . . .
I'M COMING WITH YOU.
CAMP DAKOTA
WHERE ARE WE GOING?
BACK TO MY CABIN.
WHAT FOR?
THIS!
GOOD IDEA! WE CAN USE IT TO SEE *INTO* THE ATTIC--
WHILE WE STAY *OUT* OF THE ATTIC.
CAMP DAKOTA

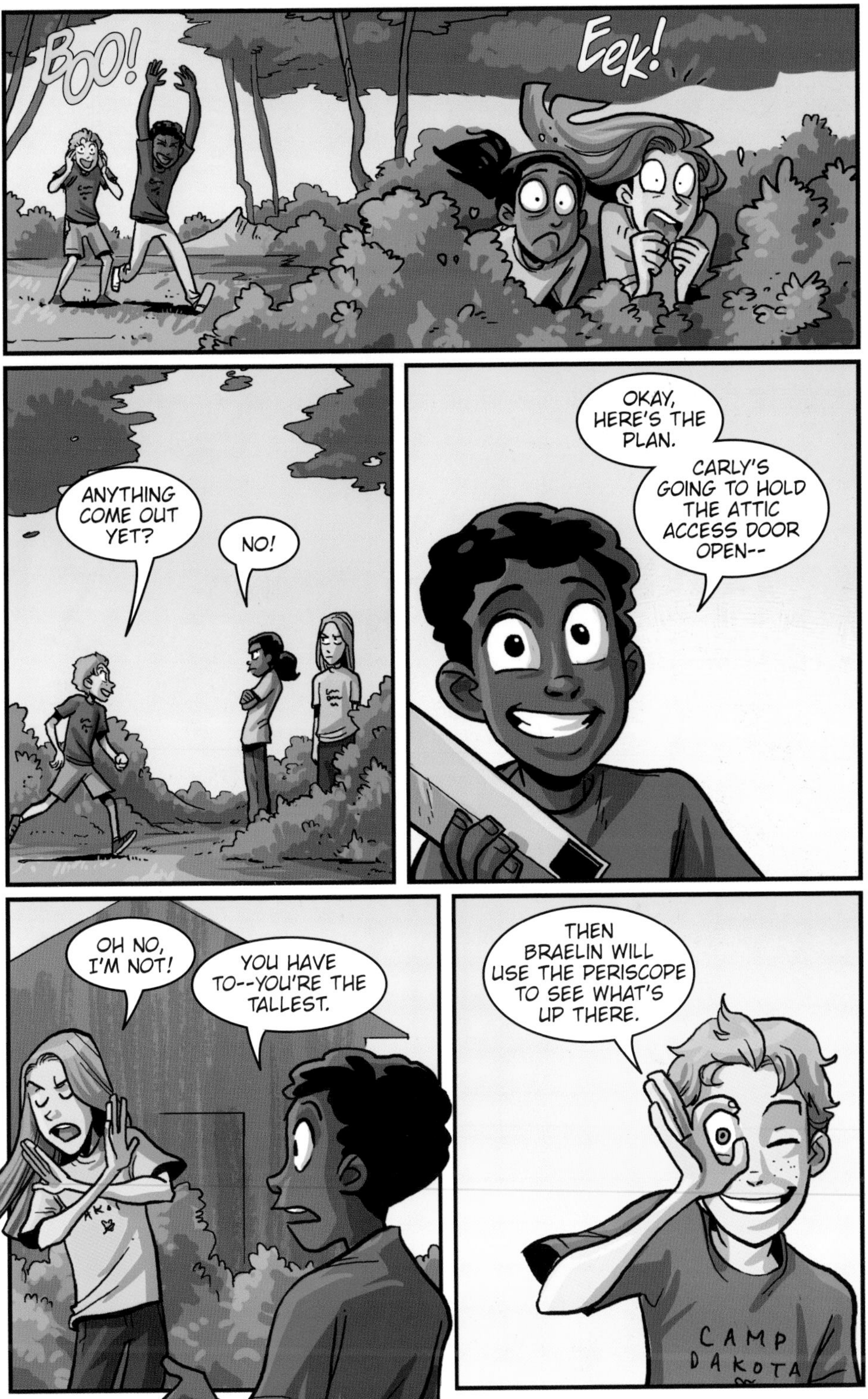
BOO!
EEK!
ANYTHING COME OUT YET?
NO!
OKAY, HERE'S THE PLAN.
CARLY'S GOING TO HOLD THE ATTIC ACCESS DOOR OPEN--
OH NO, I'M NOT!
YOU HAVE TO--YOU'RE THE TALLEST.
THEN BRAELIN WILL USE THE PERISCOPE TO SEE WHAT'S UP THERE.
CAMP DAKOTA

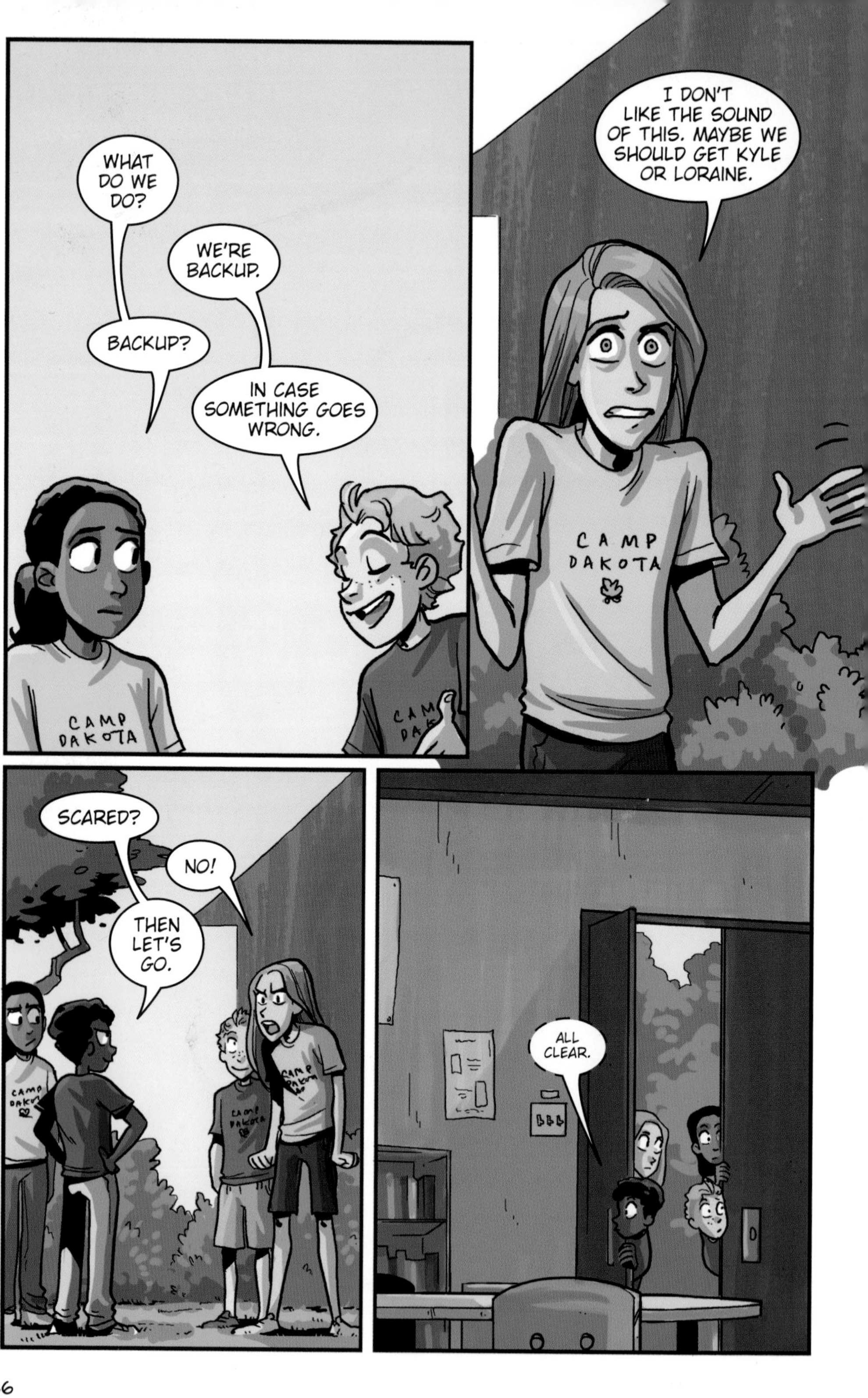
WHAT DO WE DO?
WE'RE BACKUP.
BACKUP?
IN CASE SOMETHING GOES WRONG.
CAMP DAKOTA
I DON'T LIKE THE SOUND OF THIS. MAYBE WE SHOULD GET KYLE OR LORAINE.
SCARED?
NO!
THEN LET'S GO.
ALL CLEAR.

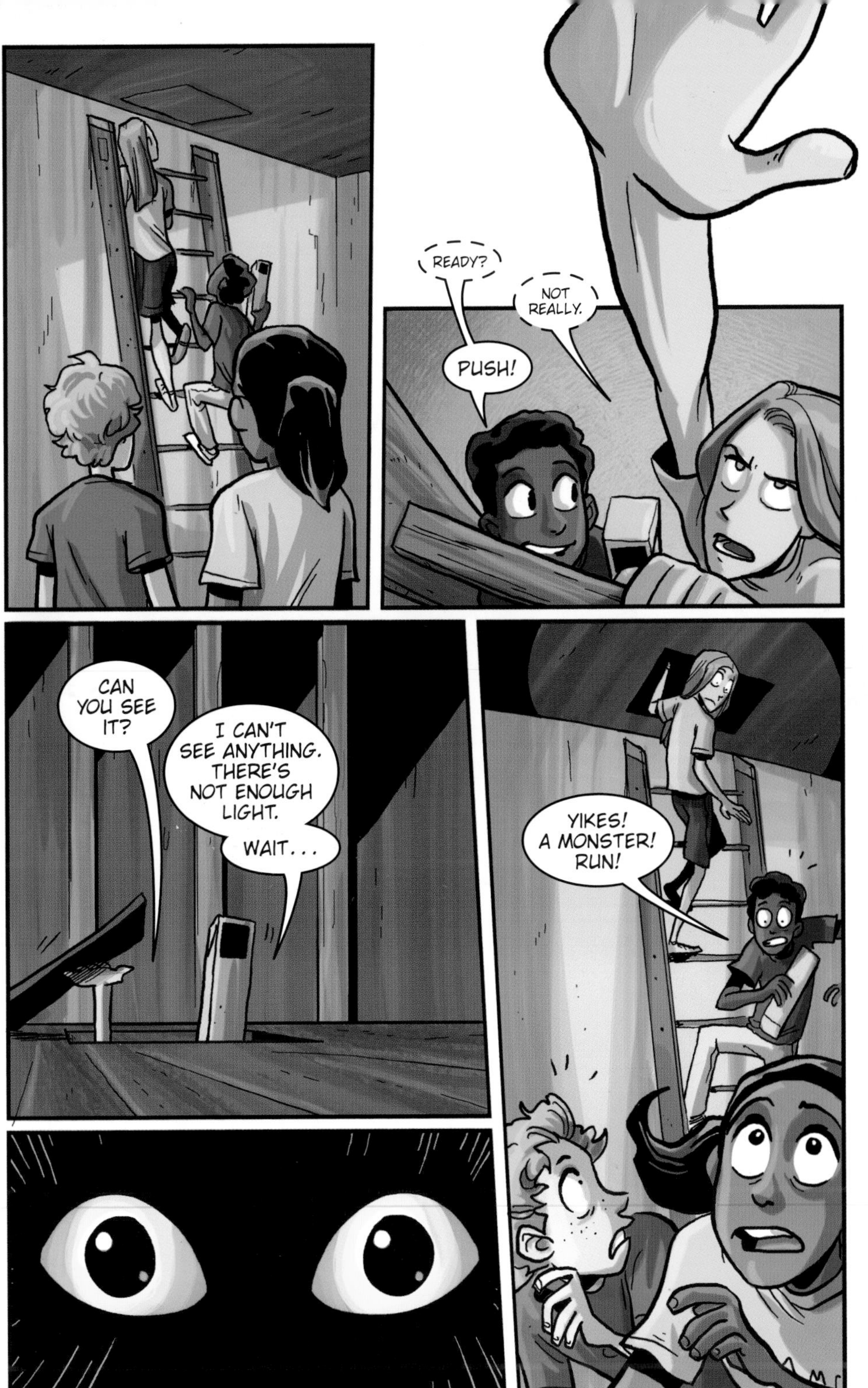
READY?
NOT REALLY.
PUSH!
CAN YOU SEE IT?
I CAN'T SEE ANYTHING. THERE'S NOT ENOUGH LIGHT.
WAIT. . .
YIKES! A MONSTER! RUN!

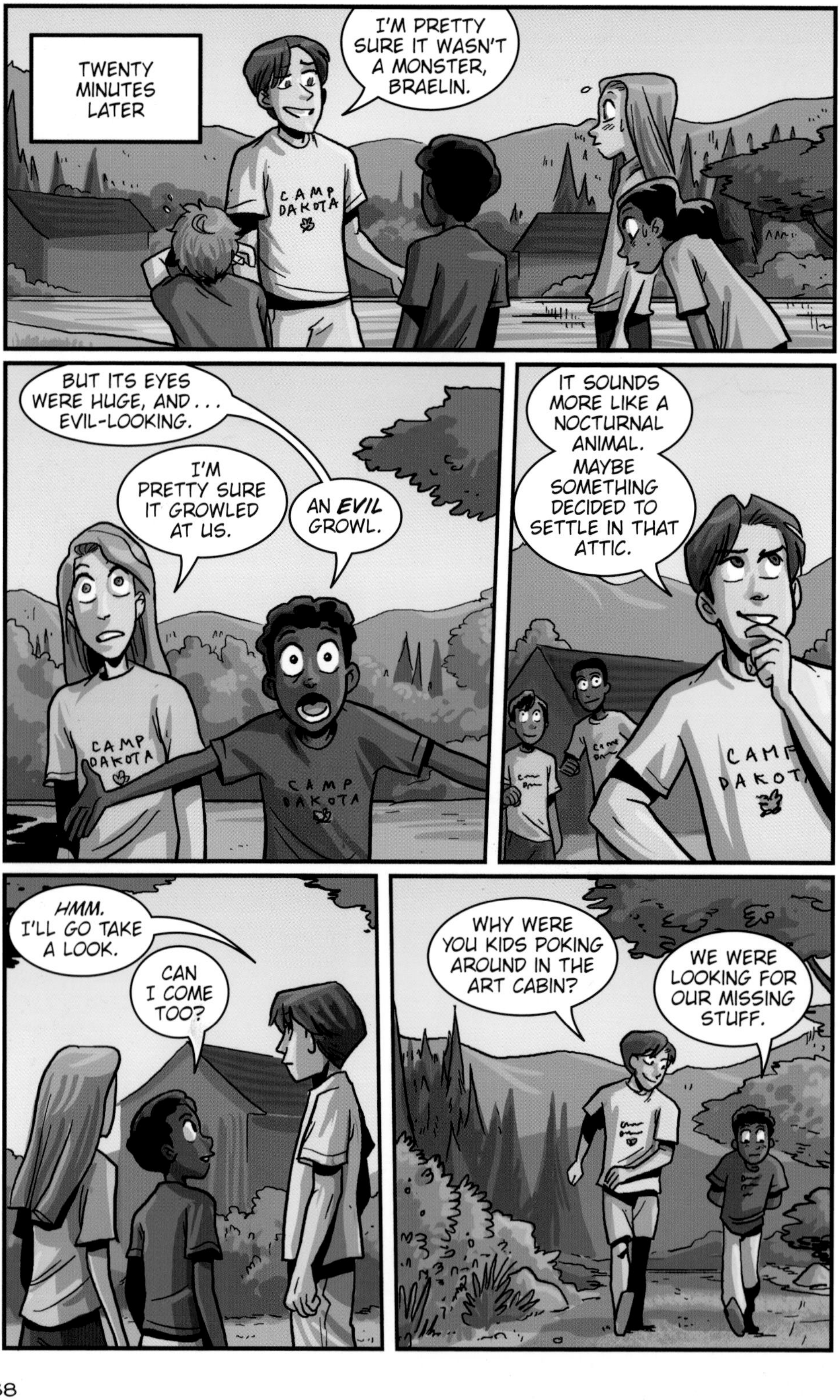
TWENTY MINUTES LATER
I'M PRETTY SURE IT WASN'T A MONSTER, BRAELIN.
CAMP DAKOTA
BUT ITS EYES WERE HUGE, AND . . . EVIL-LOOKING.
I'M PRETTY SURE IT GROWLED AT US.
AN *EVIL* GROWL.
CAMP DAKOTA
CAMP DAKOTA
IT SOUNDS MORE LIKE A NOCTURNAL ANIMAL.
MAYBE SOMETHING DECIDED TO SETTLE IN THAT ATTIC.
CAMP DAKOTA
HMM. I'LL GO TAKE A LOOK.
CAN I COME TOO?
WHY WERE YOU KIDS POKING AROUND IN THE ART CABIN?
WE WERE LOOKING FOR OUR MISSING STUFF.

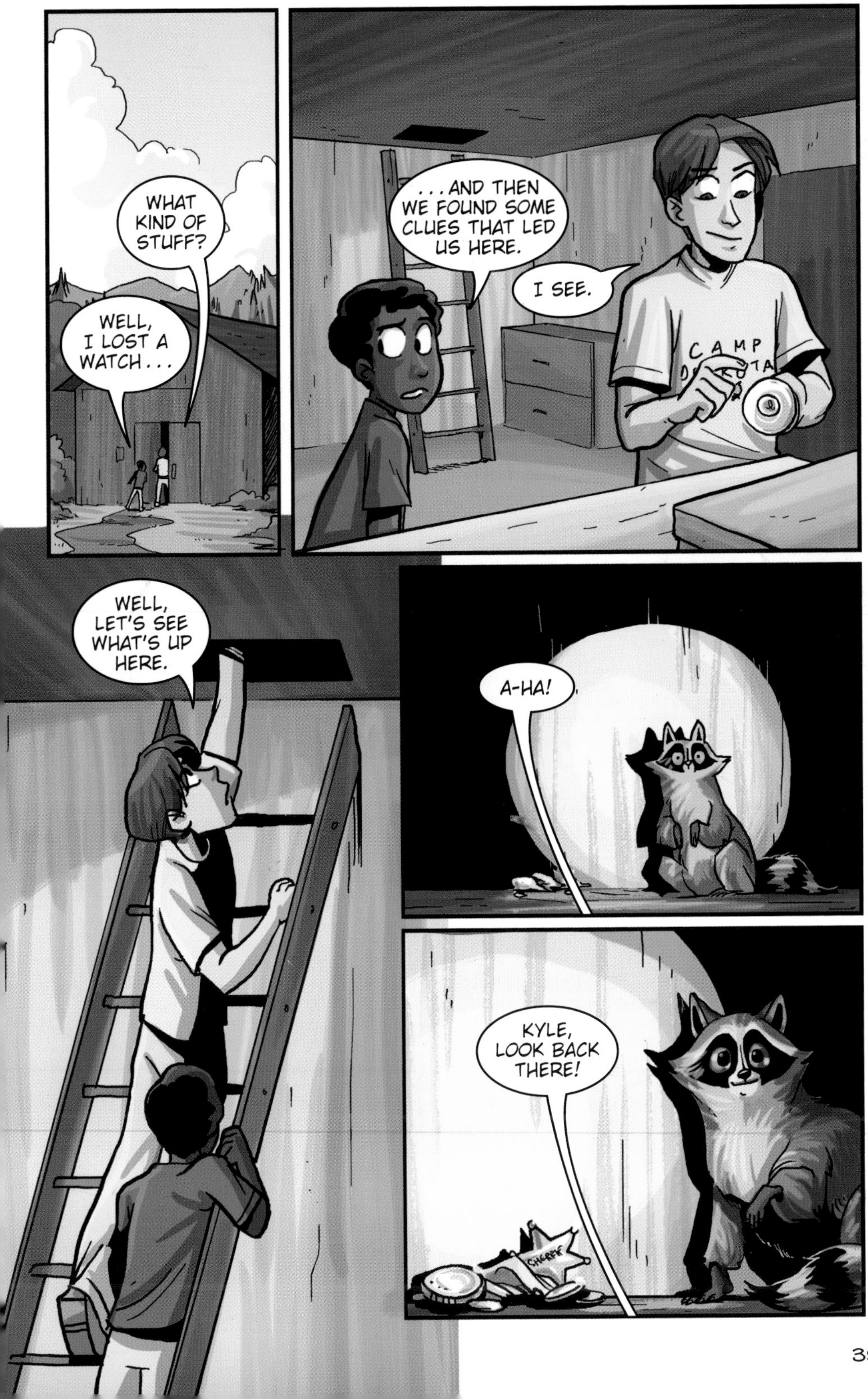
WHAT KIND OF STUFF?
WELL, I LOST A WATCH . . .
. . . AND THEN WE FOUND SOME CLUES THAT LED US HERE.
I SEE.
CAMP
WELL, LET'S SEE WHAT'S UP HERE.
A-HA!
KYLE, LOOK BACK THERE!
SHERIFF

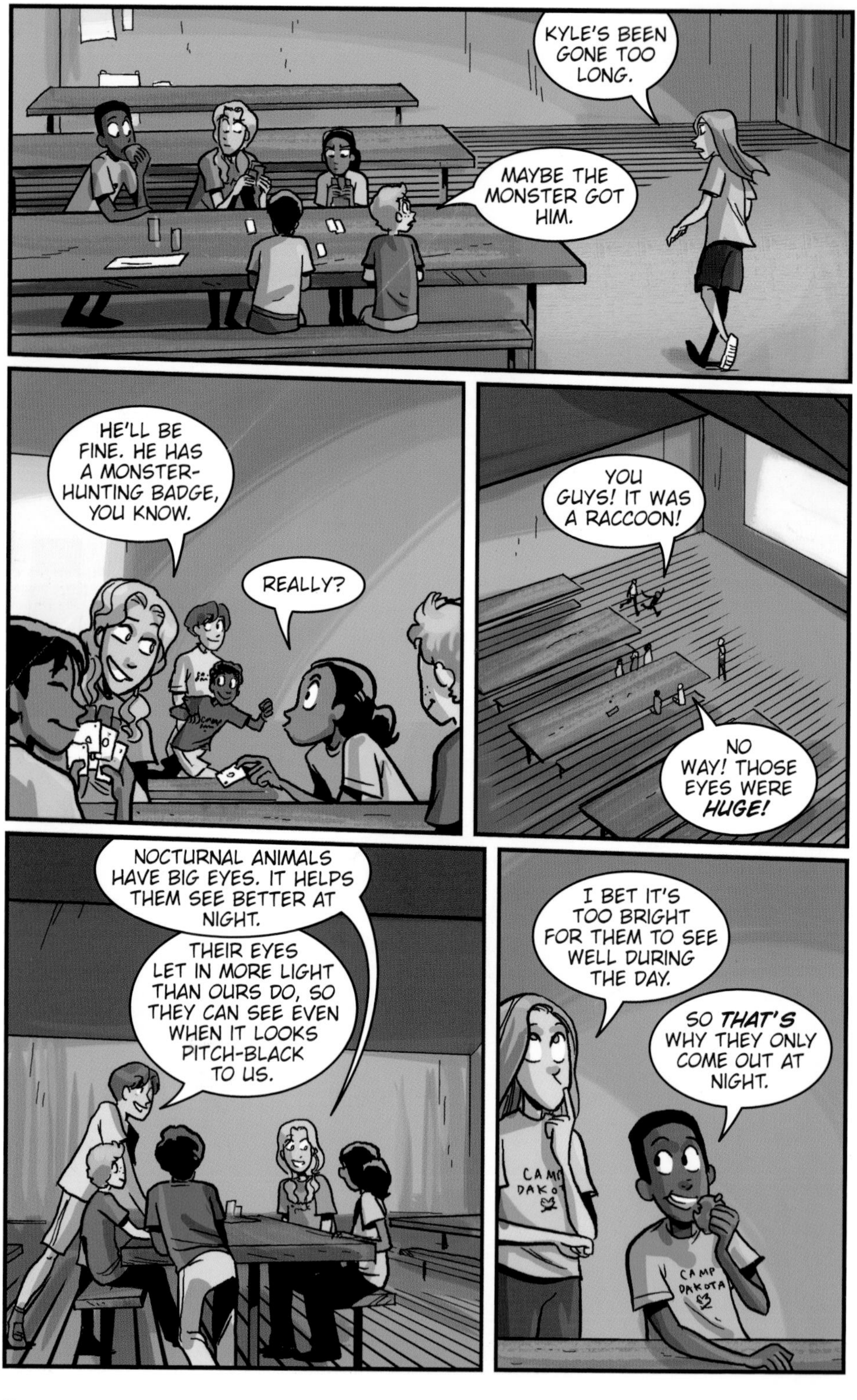
KYLE'S BEEN GONE TOO LONG.
MAYBE THE MONSTER GOT HIM.
HE'LL BE FINE. HE HAS A MONSTER-HUNTING BADGE, YOU KNOW.
REALLY?
YOU GUYS! IT WAS A RACCOON!
NO WAY! THOSE EYES WERE ***HUGE!***
NOCTURNAL ANIMALS HAVE BIG EYES. IT HELPS THEM SEE BETTER AT NIGHT.
THEIR EYES LET IN MORE LIGHT THAN OURS DO, SO THEY CAN SEE EVEN WHEN IT LOOKS PITCH-BLACK TO US.
I BET IT'S TOO BRIGHT FOR THEM TO SEE WELL DURING THE DAY.
SO ***THAT'S*** WHY THEY ONLY COME OUT AT NIGHT.
CAMP DAKOTA
CAMP DAKOTA

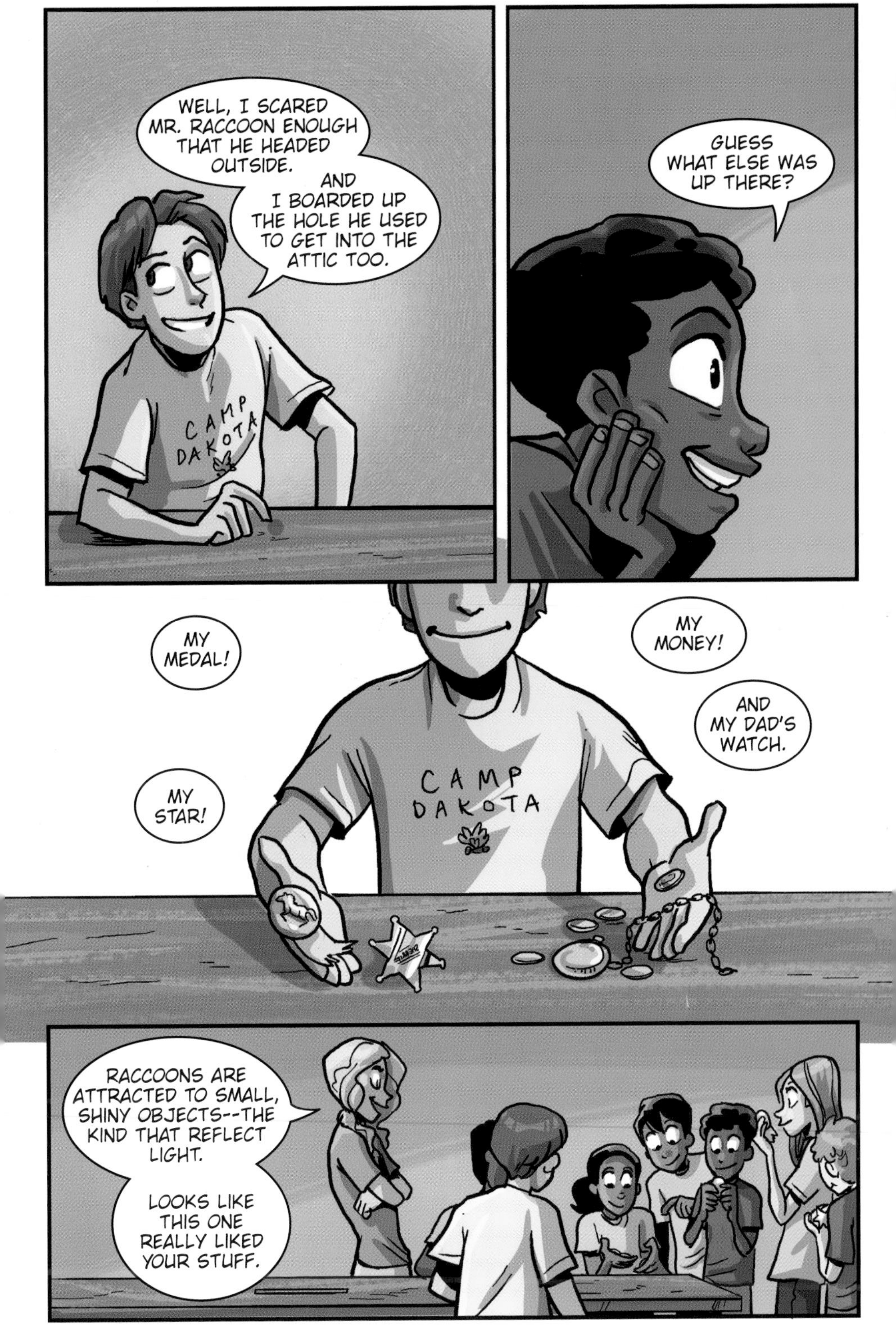
WELL, I SCARED MR. RACCOON ENOUGH THAT HE HEADED OUTSIDE.
AND I BOARDED UP THE HOLE HE USED TO GET INTO THE ATTIC TOO.
GUESS WHAT ELSE WAS UP THERE?
CAMP DAKOTA
MY MEDAL!
MY MONEY!
AND MY DAD'S WATCH.
MY STAR!
RACCOONS ARE ATTRACTED TO SMALL, SHINY OBJECTS--THE KIND THAT REFLECT LIGHT.
LOOKS LIKE THIS ONE REALLY LIKED YOUR STUFF.

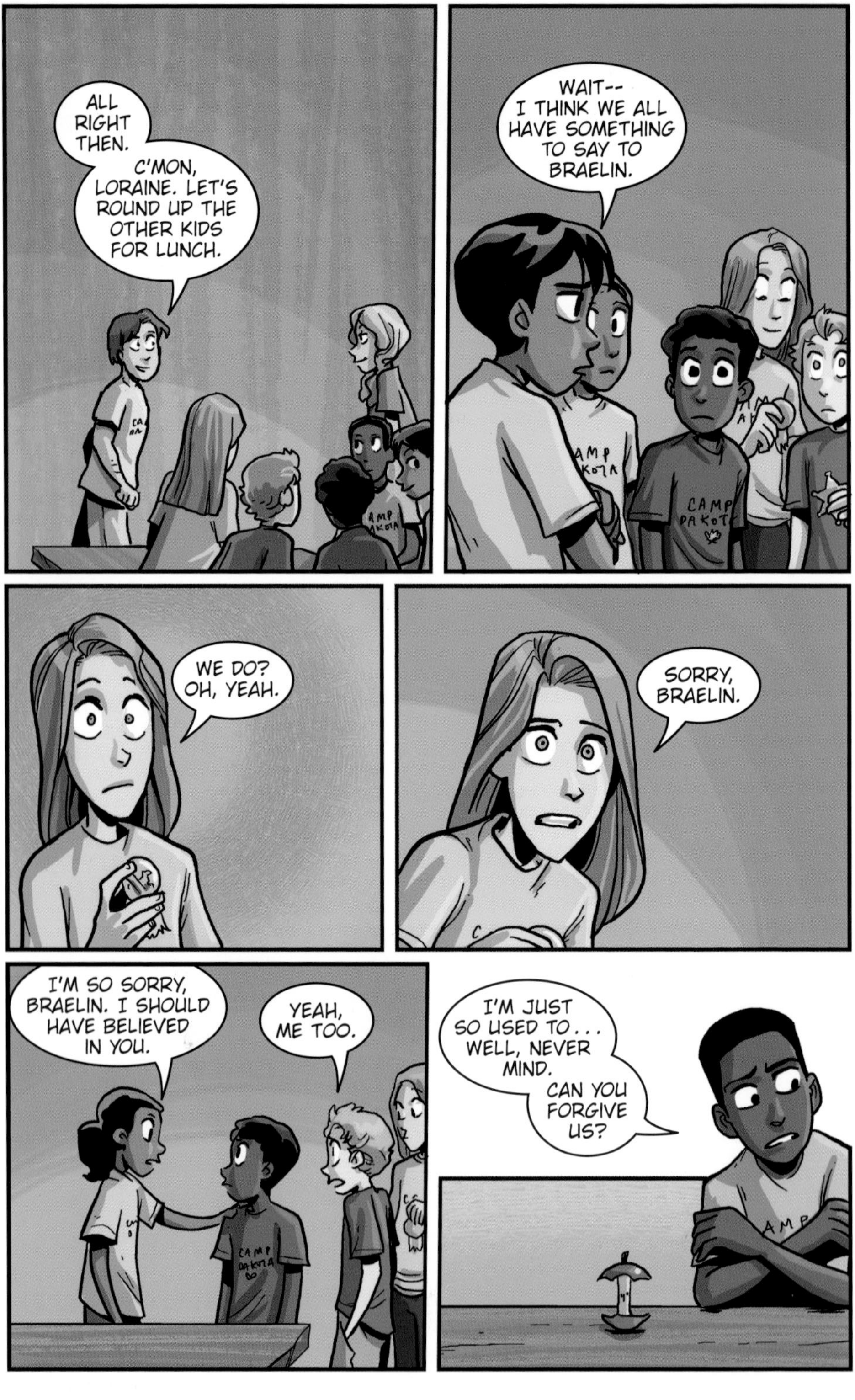
ALL RIGHT THEN.
C'MON, LORAINE. LET'S ROUND UP THE OTHER KIDS FOR LUNCH.
WAIT-- I THINK WE ALL HAVE SOMETHING TO SAY TO BRAELIN.
WE DO? OH, YEAH.
SORRY, BRAELIN.
I'M SO SORRY, BRAELIN. I SHOULD HAVE BELIEVED IN YOU.
YEAH, ME TOO.
I'M JUST SO USED TO . . . WELL, NEVER MIND.
CAN YOU FORGIVE US?

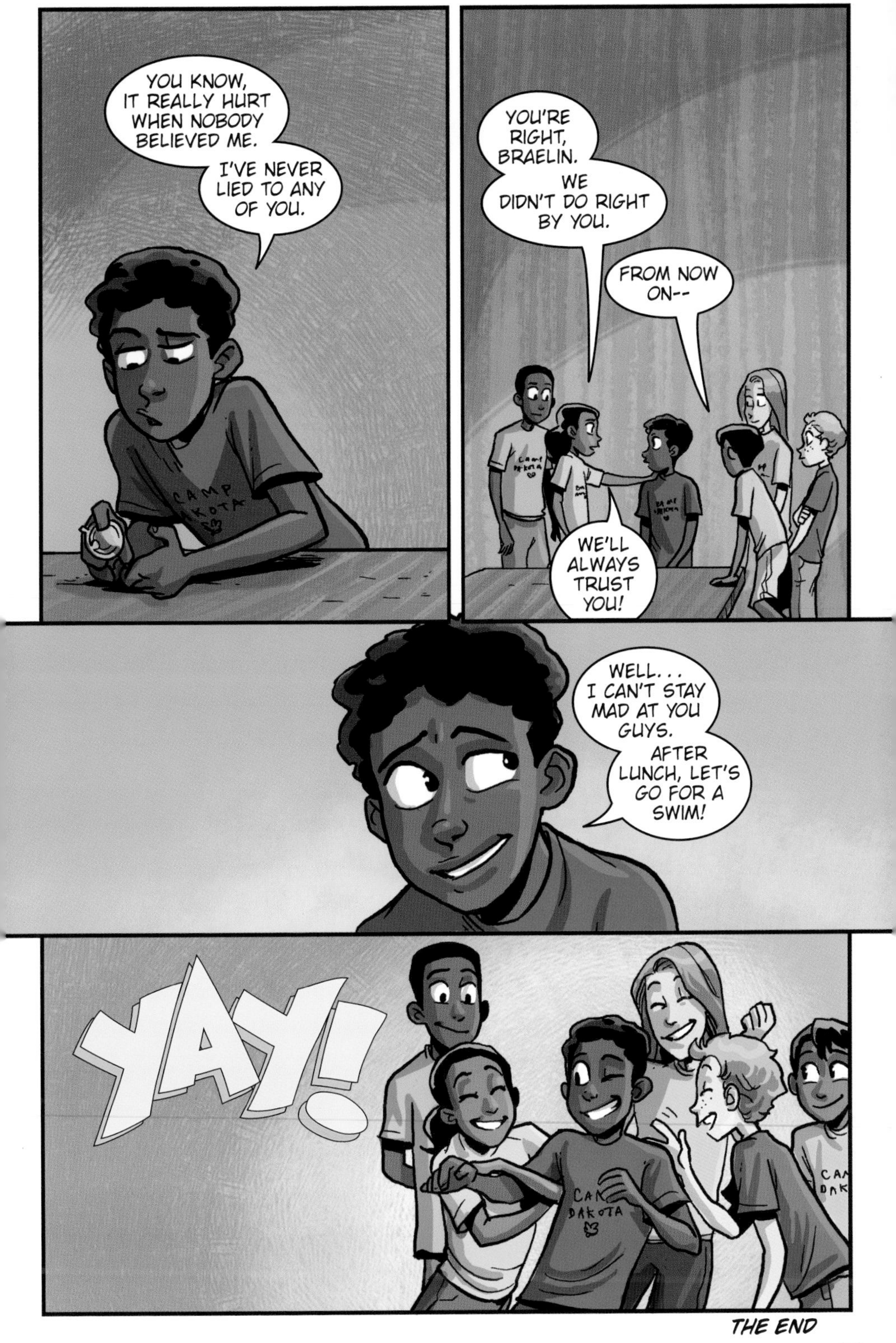
YOU KNOW, IT REALLY HURT WHEN NOBODY BELIEVED ME.
I'VE NEVER LIED TO ANY OF YOU.
YOU'RE RIGHT, BRAELIN.
WE DIDN'T DO RIGHT BY YOU.
FROM NOW ON--
WE'LL ALWAYS TRUST YOU!
WELL. . . I CAN'T STAY MAD AT YOU GUYS.
AFTER LUNCH, LET'S GO FOR A SWIM!
YAY!

THE END

Experiments

Try these fun experiments at home or in your classroom.
Make sure you have an adult help out.

Periscope

You will need: 2 (1 quart) milk cartons; scissors; 2 small, square mirrors; a utility knife (very sharp—ask an adult to help you with this); and masking or duct tape

1) Cut the tops off the milk cartons. They should now be rectangular boxes.
2) Using the scissors, cut out a square on the front side of each carton, near the bottom.
3) Lay the cartons down so that the sides with the cutout square face to the right.
4) Ask an adult to cut a short diagonal line across each carton on the side that's facing up. He or she should start near the bottom on the right side, moving up to the left. The diagonal line should be the same length as your mirrors. This will be a slot to hold the mirror in place.

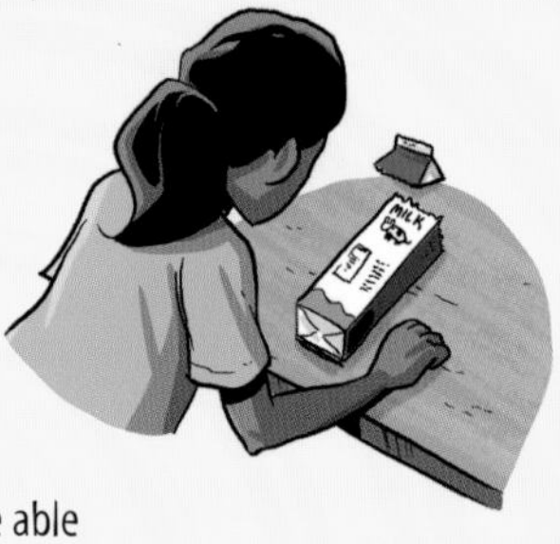
MILK

5) Slide the mirrors into the cut lines. Hold up each carton and look through the square hole. You should be able to see the ceiling.
6) Squeeze the top end of one carton so it can slide easily into the top end of the other carton. The square holes should be on opposite sides.
7) Tape the two cartons together.

How does it work?

Mirrors reflect light. Once light comes into the square hole on the top of the periscope, the first mirror reflects the light down to the second mirror. The second mirror reflects the light through the bottom square hole, reversing—and correcting—the image. Since mirrors reflect light waves exactly as they receive them, the image you see coming out of the periscope at the bottom is the same as the image that enters through the top.

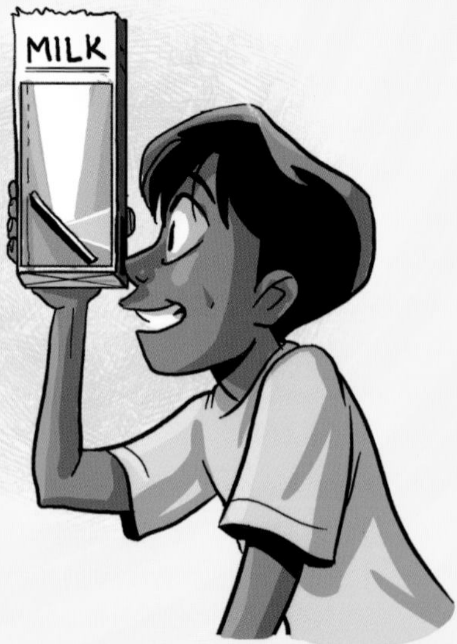
MILK

Coin Illusion

You will need: a bowl, a coin, and a large cup of water

1) Place the coin in the middle of the bowl.
2) Step back from the bowl. Keep moving back until you can no longer see the coin.
3) Stay where you are. Have someone slowly pour water from the cup into the bowl.
4) The coin will magically reappear!

How does it work?

Water refracts, or bends, light waves. Without water in the bowl, the coin is hidden by the edge of the bowl. When you add water, the light wave that carries the image of the coin becomes bent as it travels through the water. The light eventually bends enough that you can see the coin over the edge of the bowl.

Mysterious Words

density: a measure of mass per unit of volume

nocturnal: something that occurs in the night or is most active at night

periscope: an optical instrument that uses reflective surfaces such as mirrors to allow the user to see things that are not in the direct line of sight

reflection: the bouncing of light from a shiny surface

refraction: the turning or bending of light, when it passes from one medium into another that has a different density

Could YOU have solved the mystery of the cabin thief?

Good thing the kids of Camp Dakota knew a bit about light—and got some helpful tips from the counselors. See if you caught all the facts they put to use.

- Light is a form of energy. It travels in waves and moves in straight lines. When light hits an object, it either bounces (reflects) off the object or gets absorbed by it.

- All images are made of light. A person's eyes take in light. The brain then makes the light into an image that the person recognizes.

- When light hits a shiny surface, the surface reflects the waves of light in the same pattern as when it made contact. Dull surfaces do a poor job of reflecting images. These surfaces either absorb light or scatter light as it bounces off them.

- Light comes in through a periscope's top hole. It bounces off a mirror at the top toward a mirror at the bottom. Then the light travels through the periscope's bottom hole toward a viewer's eye.

- The size of an object's shadow depends on how close the object is to a light source and the angle of the light source. An object's shadow can appear much larger than the object itself.

- Raccoons are drawn to reflective surfaces. Like many other nocturnal animals, raccoons also have large eyes. Their eyes take in lots of light. This lets raccoons see well at night.

THE AUTHOR

LYNDA BEAUREGARD wrote her first story when she was seven years old and hasn't stopped writing since. She also likes teaching kids how to swim, designing websites, directing race cars out onto the track, and throwing bouncy balls for her cat, Becca. She lives near Detroit, Michigan, with her two lovely daughters, who are doing their best to turn her hair gray.

THE ARTISTS

DER-SHING HELMER graduated from University of California—Berkeley, where she played with snakes and lizards all summer long. When she is not teaching biology to high school students, she is making art and comics for everyone to enjoy. Her best friends are her two pet geckos (Smeg and Jerry), her king snake (Clarice), and the chinchilla that lives next door.

GUILLERMO MOGORRÓN started drawing before he could walk or talk. When he is not drawing monsters or spaceships piloted by monkeys, he loves to fight with his cat and walk his dog. He also enjoys meeting friends and reading comics. He lives near Madrid, Spain.

GERMAN TORRES has always loved to draw. He also likes to drive his van to the mountains and enjoy a little fresh air with his girlfriend and dogs. But what he really loves is traveling. He lives in a town near Barcelona, Spain, away from the noise of the city.